THE LAST ENEMY

A JOAN KAHN BOOK

Books by Berton Roueché

THE LAST ENEMY

By

Berton Roueché

HARPER & ROW, PUBLISHERS
New York, Evanston, San Francisco, London

A HARPER NOVEL OF SUSPENSE

FIRST U. S. EDITION

Library of Congress Cataloging in Publication Data

Roueché, Berton, 1911-
    The last enemy.
    Reprint of the ed. published by Dell Pub. Co., New York, which was issued as D90 of A Dell first edition.
    Includes index.
    I. Title.
PZ3.R753Las6 [PS3535.0845] 813'.5'4   75-6375
ISBN 0-06-013687-1

75 76 77 78 79 10 9 8 7 6 5 4 3 2 1

For
I. V. A.
and
K. E. R.

The last enemy that shall be destroyed is death.

I Corinthians XV. 26.

PROLOGUE

CORN HAD NOTHING TO FEAR. He strolled up Pine Street in the humid June morning, studying the window displays, smirking at an occasional pretty girl. Everything was under control. He turned his round, guileless, snub-nosed face this way and that, safe behind the brash and spurious look of innocence. Murder rested lightly on his disciplined conscience. It took its place with the welshed bets in Memphis, with the doctored account books in Dallas, with the muggings in Chicago and Little Rock, with the manipulated cards in New Orleans and St. Joseph and Cleveland. Murder was only Kansas City in his geography. And Kansas City was three hundred miles away. This was St. Louis.

There was a newsstand on the corner. Corn walked past, and stopped. He came slowly back. It was a waste of money. There couldn't be anything. But, of course, he had to know. Corn hated uncertainty. It was a form of untidiness. The thought brought his hand to his cheek, to the patch of gauze and tape that covered the still-tender wound. He wondered if the bandage needed changing. St. Louis was a filthy city. That was partly why he had always avoided it until now. He felt in his pocket and brought out a handful of change.

"Paper," he said.

The attendant fluttered a grimy hand. *"Post* or *Star?"*

he said. He was short and gray and he had, Corn noticed, a clubfoot.

"A paper," Corn said, with distaste.

"*Post?*" the man said.

"All right," Corn said. He stared again at the clubfoot, and covered his wince with a smile. He took the paper and dropped a nickel on the pile. "Keep the change," he said. The man didn't reply. They never did. Corn had them all buffaloed. He gave him a horselaugh, and turned away.

On the other side of the street, a crowd was gathered at a trolley stop. Corn paused on the fringe and opened the paper. The front page was all Europe and politics. He glanced without interest at a photograph of somebody flanked by a dozen microphones, and turned a page. Still nothing. He turned to the next, and there it was, at the bottom of page three. It was very short, only four paragraphs, and it contained almost nothing that hadn't been in the morning paper he had bought at the bus depot a couple of hours ago. The police were still questioning Leland Sessions. Corn smiled. The funeral would be tomorrow. Corn read on. The sheriff said he had an important clue.

Corn couldn't help chuckling. A man with a brief case under his arm and a bachelor button pinned to his lapel glanced at him coldly. Corn chuckled at the man, at the paper, at the sheriff of Jackson County. Corn had left no clues. He had left nothing, not even the three dollars in the imitation leather handbag in Louise Heim's little basement room. Corn wasn't too proud to make a dollar any way he could. In Detroit, in 1936, he had lived for five weeks by rifling pay telephones. Corn was certain that he had left nothing. And yet, there it was. He read the line again: *The sheriff said he had in his possession an important new clue.* He folded the paper under his arm. *Balls,* he thought.

A streetcar crawled up to the stop and the crowd piled in. Corn walked on, past the mirroring black glass facade of an auto loan office. He gazed darkly back at himself. His pale-gray suit was rumpled, his new white shoes were scuffed, and there was a smudge of grease on the brim of his Panama hat. The bandage, of course, was filthy. Corn frowned. That wasn't Corn. *Damn that bus,* he thought, remembering the long, sweltering night and the hiccuping drunk who had shared his seat. Damn all buses. Some day— But all he could do was straighten the necktie that had once belonged to Leland Sessions and set his jacket more firmly on his shoulders. *A clue,* he thought, *an important clue. All right,* he thought without alarm. He threw the folded paper into the gutter with the rest of the trash. Corn didn't make mistakes any more. The two instructive years at the Missouri State Reformatory at Boonville had put an end to that. *All right,* he told himself again, *we'll see.* He sent his mind ranging back to the very beginning: to February, to the Cherokee Tavern, to the three giggling girls at the bar. His instinct, as always, had been infallible. An amateur might have hesitated, but not Corn. He had known at a glance that the one in green was the one. The others had the look of a pair. She had even— There had been some remark. Corn tried to think. But he couldn't. This wasn't the place for remembering. Everything distracted him here. The girls sauntered past in their thin summer dresses. The money rolled by in the new convertibles. The luxuries beckoned from the store windows. Corn wanted a place where he could sit down. He wanted a quiet place. And a drink, he thought. Corn didn't need a drink, but he wanted one.

Halfway down the block, on Sixth Street, he found what he was looking for. There was a Lemp Beer sign over the door and a cat asleep in the window. A bar ran down one wall and there were booths along the other. Pasted on the bar mirror was a Sunday supplement photograph of Franklin Delano Roosevelt. Two men in dungarees were standing at the bar. One of them had a wrench in his hip pocket. The bartender had a boil on his neck. He looked up when Corn opened the screen door, and nodded. Corn sat down in the last booth. There was no waiter. The bartender himself brought him his glass of beer.

"Looks like another scorcher," he said.

Corn smiled at him. Honesty and good fellowship shone in the blue eyes, the snub nose, the round pink cheeks.

"You said that right," he said.

"Paper said we might get some rain," the bartender said.

"I reckon we could use it," Corn said.

The bartender looked thoughtfully at the wall. But he had nothing more to say. Corn waited until he turned away, and then took a swallow of his beer. It wasn't cold, but it tasted good. He loosened Leland Sessions's necktie and lighted a cigarette and put his feet up on the opposite seat. He had established residence in St. Louis. He was ready to remember Louise Heim.

She had telephoned him, as he had known she would, the next evening. She had called him at the shoeshine parlor on East Twelfth Street where his name was Wheeler, where he was believed to follow one of the smaller floating crap games. His name was Martin at the bar on Wyandotte Street where he loitered through his afternoons. It was the impression there that he had some kind of job with the city. At the rooming-house where he was living that month, his name was Lake and he worked on the night shift at the Power & Light Company. Louise thought he worked for one of the juke box syndicates. She didn't know where he lived. He never told anybody that. He sometimes hardly knew himself. Corn moved regularly every couple of weeks, and sometimes more often than that. He was always the new roomer, or the man who had checked out the day before. It was the secret of his survival. Corn didn't believe in taking chances, not even at craps or cards. Corn believed in anticipating the end at the beginning.

Sitting at ease in the cool gloom of the Sixth Street bar, Corn had to admit that he hadn't quite anticipated the end of Louise Heim. There had been no precedent for that. But he had known that her life with Corn was limited.

And he had taken all of the usual precautions. They had met, that first night, in the lobby of the Pickwick Hotel. Corn had chosen the place. It adjoined the biggest and busiest bus depot. So did the restaurant, where he had held her chair and lighted her cigarettes and ordered the six-course dinner and talked as only Corn knew how. He had also selected the movie and the bar, and the nameless walk-up hotel. Corn had been the last, but he hadn't been the first. He sipped his beer and smiled at the stamped-tin ceiling overhead, remembering the long and rambling apology for a hardware clerk in Harrisonville. In the big brass bed, she had sobbed out her happiness and her gratitude for tolerance, clutching the shoulder that she had bitten only half an hour before. "Rex, honey, you're just about the sweetest thing . . ."

Corn scratched a match on his thumbnail and lighted another cigarette, and thought of the funeral tomorrow. He had been her only friend, but he wouldn't be there. But there had been so many others: the high school girl in New Orleans, the Indian girl in Tulsa, the Mexican in Houston, the tortured wife in Hot Springs, and all the other girls and wives and sweethearts in Memphis and Dallas and Omaha and all the other places. Sentiment couldn't touch him any more. The years stood in the way, and the cold furnished room in Joplin, with his mother threshing beneath the damp blankets and the intern who had arrived too late and the terror of incomprehension that fastened him stricken beside the fernery while somebody tried to explain and somebody promised him candy. Sentiment was that crowded empty room, and he could never go back. Even his memory couldn't reach it. He had left that past behind him when he left the settlement house.

Louise had also left the past behind. Except for the clerk in Harrisonville, she had none. Her life had begun two years ago. She arrived in the city in the morning. She was at the employment agency by noon. That night, she was a maid in the home of Mrs. Arthur Sessions, with a room of her own in the basement and an area entrance that opened on a corner of the garden. Corn strolled by one February afternoon and studied the deep lawn, the sheltering plantations of evergreen, the thick garden shrubbery. Corn was cautious, but he wasn't made of money. Even the walk-up cost a dollar. He was satisfied.

Two nights later, he was there. She opened the door at his signal, shaking with love and panic, but there was really nothing to fear. The living-room was directly overhead and the cook slept in the other wing, in a large room off the kitchen. That night as it happened, was the only night they had even had a scare. Corn was unbuttoning her uniform when they heard steps on the basement stairs. He was in the closet before they reached the bottom. It was Sophie, the cook, sent by Mrs. Sessions with a message about something tomorrow. She stayed only long enough to catch her breath for the climb back up the stairs. Louise reacted from fright with an almost overwhelming passion. Corn crept wearily out at dawn, with four packages of Leland Sessions's cigarettes and a borrowed dollar.

Those were the days, Corn thought without regret. It all seemed long ago. Louise had wanted him there every night. She yearned for domesticity, and the bare little basement room was their home. The great, unwieldly walnut rocker was Corn's chair. "Even when I'm here alone," she told him one night, "I wouldn't think of sitting in it." She moved closer to him on the white metal bed, gravely confessing everything. "Sometimes, when you have to work nights, I sit here by myself and pretend you're in your chair." Corn smirked at her, and picked his nose. Devotion was only what he expected. In return, he was willing to listen. He poured himself another drink of the Sessionses' whisky.

"I even talk to it sometimes," Louise said. "Just like I talk to you, Rex, honey. Our private talk."

"Do you, baby?" he said.

Now, remembering, he had a flicker of uneasiness. He wondered if it had been wise to tell her his real given name. But pride had triumphed over caution.

"You know what it means?" he had asked her. "My name —Rex? It means 'King.' I guess you didn't know that."

Corn put that worry away. It couldn't make any difference now. But the moment of doubt had broken his train of thought. He glanced across the room. The bartender and the two men in dungarees were howling with laughter. They had been joined by a man in shirt sleeves and a straw hat with a colored band. He was grinning modestly.

"That's what I told him," he said. "I guess I sure enough told him off."

Corn relaxed in his booth. The world was full of squares. Everything was easy for Corn. But the sheriff's clue still hung in his mind, and Corn was thorough. He drifted confidently back to the basement room and poked reflectively among the ruins. Assurance was everywhere his memory turned. No one had even seen him anywhere with Louise Heim. They had never, after that first night, been anywhere together. Corn had made sure of that. It was as though he had had a premonition, like the inner warning that had kept him away from the poker game in Denver on the night of the big raid, that had impelled him to leave Little Rock the day before Johnny Ralph was picked up, that had told him to avoid the fatuous drunk in the Dearborn Station in Chicago who had turned out to be a city detective when somebody else tried to take him over. Corn had a seventh sense.

But there had been no warning that last night. Corn stared at his warm beer and remembered the beginning of the end. Last Friday night had begun like every other night. He had dropped off the streetcar at the usual stop at the usual time, and, as usual, halted at the mailbox by the darkened drugstore on the corner and lighted a cigarette. He then, as always, crossed the street and headed north. In the distance hung the sky-high lights of the mesa of new apartments on the hill. With his jacket over his arm and his hat on the back of his head, he might have been a night worker hurrying home. But at the next corner, he turned to the right, away from the hill, and at the next, he turned right again. That brought him to Aberdeen Road. There were no shops here and no apartments, and even the houses were few and far between. With every block, they drew farther apart and deeper into their broad and wooded lawns. The only lights were street lights and the only sound was the night. Corn discarded his cigarette. He had to be careful now. The Sessions house was just ahead, a glimmer of whitewashed brick in a breathless frame of foliage. Corn hesitated and glanced back the way he had come. Then he glided behind the great, silent sycamore, behind the cloaked evergreens that stood as stiff as monuments, across the rustling gravel drive, and into the sheltered garden. He felt for the wrought-iron railing that marked the area entrance, and ducked quickly down the black, familiar steps. He tapped his signal on the heavy door and waited, silently whistling the nameless tune that always brought him luck.

The door came open at once. Louise, as usual, had been waiting. She peered blindly out at the night. She had pale-blue eyes and pale-red hair, and she was tightly wrapped in a pale-green bathrobe.

"Rex," she whispered. "Oh, honey. I was almost afraid you weren't coming."

Corn smiled. She was well trained. He liked a worried welcome.

"Were you, baby?" he said.

He gave her a rewarding slap on the bottom. Louise collapsed in his arms. Her mouth was damp with fresh lipstick. She began to groan with what could have been either dismay or delight.

"Hey," Corn said. "Watch yourself. This is a clean shirt."

They moved across the concrete floor, past the dark bulk of the furnace, and under the labyrinth of pipes. A bicycle with two flat tires leaned against a tier of crates. Overhead, the house gave a sleepy creak.

Corn said, "Did you get me some handkerchiefs?"

"I only could get just one," Louise said. "But it's real pretty, honey. Oh, golly, Rex, I'm so glad you—"

"One?" Corn said. "That's just dandy. I hope you at least had sense enough to get one without any initial this time. I had to throw three of those others away."

"I know," she said. "I got a nice plain one. No initial or anything." She followed him into her room and closed the door. She gazed at him with love and longing. "Oh, honey, I just don't know what I'd have done if you hadn't come tonight."

"Feeling lonely, baby?" Corn said. He smirked. "Me, too." He tossed his jacket on a chair and loosened his necktie. "How about cigarettes?"

"Umm," Louise said. She went over to the white bureau in the corner and picked up a package of Camels. "I got you two packs," she said. "He's changed to Camels, though. You don't mind Camels, do you, honey?"

Corn stretched. "They're okay," he said. "Anything's better than the ones I've been smoking. They were beginning to get my throat."

Louise came over to the bed. She sat down beside him and began to open the package. The top of her bathrobe fell open. Beneath it, she was naked. Corn cupped a long, pale breast in his hand. He gazed at it judiciously.

"I feel good," he said, and yawned.

"I'm glad," she said. "So do I, except—"

"Here!" Corn said. "Give me those cigarettes. You'll tear the whole top off that way."

"No, I won't," she said. "See?" She shook a cigarette loose, put it between his lips, and lighted it. She dropped the match in the tray on the night table.

Corn withdrew his hand from her breast. He was in no hurry. They had all night. He lay back and blew a plume of smoke at the ceiling.

Louise adjusted the front of her robe and watched him, smiling an uncertain smile.

"Well?" he remarked.

She continued to look at him.

"Well?" he said again. "You act like you never saw me before. How do I look?"

Louise started. "What?" she said. "Why—why, you look wonderful." She sighed. "You always look wonderful to me, honey."

Corn let his smile fade. "To you?" he said. "Thanks for the compliment."

"Honey," she said. "You know that wasn't what I meant. I just—"

"All right," Corn said. He sat up and took the package of cigarettes from her lap and put it carefully on the table. "All right. Then what's eating you? Has the old bitch been riding you again?"

"Sophie?" Louise said. It was as though she had to stop and think. She shook her head uneasily. "No. It isn't her. It isn't anything like—"

"Well?" Corn said.

"It's something else. I—" Her mouth began to tremble. "Honey. Oh, Rex. I'm so scared."

Corn swung his feet to the floor. He pulled her chin around. The robe fell open again and the long breasts quivered and swayed. But this time he didn't notice. "Look," he said. "I feel good tonight. But I'm getting tired of this crap. I don't like mysteries."

She tried to smile. "I know," she said. "I—"

Corn had an inspiration. He said, "Don't tell me that Sessions punk—" He almost laughed. "Has the boy banker been trying to get funny?"

She was shocked. "Honey!" she said. "Don't talk like that. Even in fun. As if I'd— Besides, he hardly knows I'm alive." She looked at him with yearning. "I just don't know how to say it."

"Okay," he said. "Then forget it. Or write me a letter sometime." He pulled his necktie over his head and hung it on the bedpost. He began to unbutton his shirt. "I feel like playing."

"No," she said. "Wait." She put her hand on his wrist. "Wait, honey. I'll tell you. I want to tell you. Only promise me. Tell me you won't get mad?"

"Mad?" Corn said. His hand came away from his shirt.

She suddenly began to cry. The breasts lurched. She fell heavily into his arms. She said, "Honey, we're—" She hid her face and whimpered. "We're going to have to get married."

Corn pushed her away from him, violently. It was like an act of self-defense. He might have been warding off a blow. He stared at her.

She said miserably, "I love you so much." It was as if that explained everything. "And you're not mad. Are you, honey? Please don't be mad."

Corn stood up. He looked down at her with revulsion. Marriage was the bleak furnished room in Joplin. It was the couple wrangling on the floor below. It was the bed thumping on Saturday night. He could hardly trust himself to speak.

"Are you crazy?" he said.

Louise gave a kind of wail, and began to cry again. The tears streaked down her cheeks like wrinkles. She seemed to be aging before his eyes.

He said furiously, "Stop blubbering!" He put out a hand and caught her by the shoulder. "I said shut up." He shook her. "Shut up and tell me just what the hell this is all about."

She raised her head. "We've got to get married." She swallowed. "I'm pregnant. I'm going to have a baby."

Corn turned away. He had himself in hand now. He plucked a cigarette from the package on the table and slowly struck a match. "Yeah?" he said. "And what makes you think that, baby?"

"I know," she said. "I know I am. I wasn't sure at first. That's why I didn't say anything. But I am now. Honey, don't be—"

She flung herself on him.

"Please tell me you aren't mad." She tried to find his mouth. "I know how you feel. I really do. And I didn't mean to. You know I didn't mean to. But I'll be a good wife, honey. I'll make you happy. I'll do everything I—"

Corn jerked himself free.

"God damn it," he said. "Get off of me. And shut up. You want to wake up the whole block?"

"I knew you'd be mad." She fumbled in her pocket for a handkerchief. She dabbed her reddened eyes. "But, honey —I had to tell you. And I waited until I was absolutely certain it—"

"Sure," Corn said. "So you finally went to the doctor, and he—" He smirked.

She thought it was a smile. She thought he meant it. "No," she said. "I mean, not yet. But if you—" She looked at him with hope.

"No," Corn said. "I didn't suppose you had." He chuckled. Then he said sharply, "Okay, baby. You've got a good act. A lot of guys would have fallen for it. Harrisonville or wherever you're from is probably full of them. But not me. So forget it." He watched her mouth fall open. "Or shall I be on my way?"

He began to button up his shirt.

"Rex!" Her eyes went wide with incredulity. The balled handkerchief dropped from her hand.

"I don't know what you mean. Where are you going? You can't go. You can't—"

"Okay," Corn said. "I'll stay, then. I'm in a good mood tonight. I'll forget all about that hickory act." He grinned at her. "But frankly, baby, I never dreamed you'd try anything like that on me. I really gave you more credit."

She gave a frightened cry. The red eyes blinked at him with a kind of panic.

"Rex," she said. "Rex, honey. I don't know what you mean. I don't understand."

Corn said nothing. He drew on his cigarette and watched the conflict in the thin, streaked face. Incomprehension struggled, and gave way. Truth stepped rudely in. He could almost feel the jar.

Louise said slowly, "Don't—don't you believe me? Don't you believe me, Rex?"

"Frankly," he said, "I—"

"*Rex!*"

Suddenly he was angry. It wasn't funny any more. The joke was over. He slapped her hard across the face.

"Shut up," he said. He jabbed his cigarette into the ash tray. "I told you to quit yelling. I don't want the whole house in on this."

"You don't believe me," she said faintly. "You think I'm —you think it's just a trick."

Corn raised his eyebrows. "What a brain!" he said. "She actually understands the English language."

"You don't believe me," she said again.

"Frankly," Corn said, "it doesn't make any difference whether I believe you or not. I don't like—"

"But I'm going to have a baby." She backed slowly away toward the bureau. She said, "Your baby."

Corn buttoned the collar of his shirt.

"Is it?" he said. "What makes you think so? I mean, just supposing you are knocked up."

"You're joking," she said with one last crumb of hope. "You're only trying to scare me."

Corn stepped past her to the mirror. He worked the knot of Leland Sessions's necktie carefully into place. Sessions was a jerk. All the money in the world, but instead of enjoying life, he buried himself in a bank. And not just for kicks. Apparently, he really worked at it. How square, Corn wondered, could you get? But he had to give him credit. He had good taste in ties.

"Rex," Louise said. "Honey—listen. Look at me."

Corn turned. "You look at me," he said. "Look at this shirt. I ought to— It was clean two hours ago."

"I know," she said. "But you *are* just trying to scare me, aren't you? Aren't you, Rex?"

Corn walked back to the chair where his jacket lay.

"Am I?" he said. "It looks to me like what I'm doing is leaving. Doesn't it look that way to you?"

He started to pick up his jacket, and remembered the cigarettes. One package was on the table. The other was on the bureau. As he moved toward the table, he heard the scrape of a drawer. The secret warning flashed in his mind. He wheeled around.

Louise stood backed against the bureau. The robe hung open, from the dancing breasts to the thick thighs, and her eyes were glazed. She was breathing through her mouth, and trembling. It might have been lust. But it wasn't. In her right hand was a pair of long-bladed shears.

"What do you think you're doing?" Corn said. "Put those scissors down. You've caused enough trouble for one night."

Louise said, "You're not going to leave me. Not until you promise. I was telling you the truth. And there hasn't been anybody else. Not since—"

Corn said, "Put those damn things down. You hear me?"

"Not until you promise," she said. She choked. "You can't—"

"You heard me," he said. He took a step toward her. "Am I going to have to—"

He wasn't prepared when she moved. Women always did what Corn told them to do. There had been no reason to think she was any different from the others. He saw her arm go up, and reached for it. But he was half a second too late. There was a flash of brightness past his eyes. For an instant he had no sense of pain. For an instant he was only startled. Then something warm and salty touched the corner of his mouth, and his cheek began to burn.

Louise struck at him again. But this time he was ready. His fingers closed around her wrist. He was holding her arm, twisting it down and away, when the pain exploded in his face. It was all he could do to keep his fingers biting into her wrist.

He heard her cry, "I gave you every nickel I had. You made me steal—" And then she screamed.

Corn said, "Shut up." The pain brought tears to his eyes. "God damn your big—"

He stopped. It was as if they had been struggling in the dark and the lights had abruptly come on. For the first time he saw the shears in his own hand. Louise lay sprawled on the bed in a tangle of green robe. There was a long black tear in her throat. From it rose a throbbing flow of blood.

"Louise," he said, staring down at the welling blood and the long dark tear. She didn't move. "Baby," he said. It was impossible that anyone could endure such a wound in silence. But there was no sound save the pant of his own breathing. There was no sound anywhere.

Then, suddenly, in his mind, he heard her scream again. It was like a siren. It ran shrieking up and down the room, echoing from wall to wall. The pain of his wound vanished, as though it had been miraculously healed. The echoing scream dinned in his ears. Corn was in danger. He threw the shears onto the bed. The tiny thump thundered through the room. He rushed to the door. Corn was wounded and in danger. He wrenched at the knob. It wouldn't open. Sweat streamed down his face and pain revived. The door was stuck or locked or— He had been turning the knob the wrong way. He flung himself through, and stopped. Corn was in danger, but he was no fool. Standing rigid and intent, he listened. Nothing stirred.

There wasn't a sound. He listened again. It was possible that no one had heard. It was possible that the scream had died beyond the door, that it hadn't pierced the solid flooring and the expensive, well-hung doors. She had only screamed once.

Corn backed into the room and closed the door. The thought of his panic was harder to bear than the pain in his cheek. Corn had almost left the police his jacket, his matches, and his fingerprints. Corn had never had so great a need for thoroughness. He stood by the door for an instant, sick with his folly, trying to calm himself. Then he walked over to the bed, circling around the blood that was puddled on the floor. He felt nothing but the pain in his cheek and a kind of relief. He hadn't been simple enough to run. There wasn't time for remorse. It was as though he had never known Louise Heim, as though a stranger lay on the bed. He looked down at her, at the torn and blood-ied robe, at the dark pool beneath the pale-red hair. No one could survive such a wound. But she might be only dying. She might revive.

Someone might find her before death finally closed in. *I better make sure,* he thought. Corn couldn't take any chances now. He picked up a pillow and pressed it over her face. He held it there and counted slowly to three hundred.

Corn then went methodically to work. He might have been born for murder. With the case of the other pillow, he wiped the shears clean and dropped them in the pool beneath the bed. He wiped the ash tray, the table and the chairs, and the knob of the door. He put the matches and the two packages of cigarettes into his coat pocket. Then he put the pillowcase back on the pillow. He glanced care-fully around the room to make sure he had missed noth-ing.

A pocketbook on the bureau caught his eye. He cov-ered his hands with his handkerchief and opened it. In the coin purse he found three dollars in currency and some change. He put the bills in his pocket, but he left the rest. It mustn't look like robbery.

Corn had almost forgotten his wound. Now, at the bureau, he studied it in the wavering glass. It wasn't as bad as he had thought. There was no blood on his hands. There was none on his trousers or on his shoes. Corn's luck was holding. There were two small smears on his shirt sleeve, but his jacket would cover that. He gazed at himself again and wiped his cheek with his handkerchief. *It can't be much,* he told himself. *It's almost stopped bleed-ing already.* The fine white handkerchief with the blue, hand-turned border that Louise had taken from Leland Sessions's drawer lay on the bureau. Corn shook loose the folds and crumpled it in his hand. He wiped his damp forehead with it. He blew his nose. He dropped it onto the floor and rocked his foot over it. He picked it up, walked across the room, and dropped it beside the bed. It would be something for the police to find. If Louise had been lying, if Mister Sessions had ever so much as— Corn smiled. He didn't wish him any hard luck. But Corn had to look out for himself.

Corn put on his coat and hat. He left the light on and the door half open. He wiped the knob again with his handkerchief and crept quietly through the shadows to the entryway. There was a snap lock on the area door. Corn wrapped his hand in his handkerchief and opened it. He went through and the door closed with a sigh and a click, locked on the inside. He put his handkerchief back into his pocket and slipped up the dark steps and under the sheltering trees. When he reached the sidewalk, he walked fast. He wondered if it was wisdom or panic. But it would hardly be prudent to loiter. His heart thumped at every crossing, at every rustle in the shrubbery, at every stir of the night. Corn was used to the security of doorways and the safety of alleys. He wanted the anonymity of crowds. A block from the boulevard, he turned east. He couldn't risk the usual streetcar tonight. He had to find another line. Walking through the silent, empty, endless blocks, trailed by the tap of his heels, Corn told himself that he had lost nothing of value. He had sacrificed a few cigarettes, a few dollars, a few more neckties and handkerchiefs. He had planned to move on anyway, in July or August at the latest. It never occurred to him to wonder if she had actually been pregnant. Corn never wasted time on conjecture. He saved his wits for survival.

It was almost three o'clock when he reached the safety of a suburban shopping center. His spirits lifted among the all-night cafés and the drugstores, the people and the parked cars, the neon and the noise. He waited at the car stop, fanning himself with his hat, shielding the evidence on his cheek. On the streetcar, he covered the wound with his hand and pretended to be trying to sleep. At four-fifteen he dragged himself up the stairs to his room on Washington Street.

Corn had had a strenuous night. He fell on his bed and closed his eyes. When he opened them again, it was afternoon. Somebody had left a Saturday paper in the bathroom. But it was the morning paper, and there was nothing in it. He went back to his room and lay down for another hour.

The shouts of the newsboys followed him down Twelfth Street when he went cautiously out to breakfast, and the headlines stared from the stands. He read the stories in the two papers while he ate among the harried lunch-hour crowds. Everybody at the counter was reading. Everybody had his theory. The police were questioning everyone: Mrs. Sessions, Leland Sessions, Sophie Binder, the neighborhood watchman. Mrs. Binder had heard a scream—or thought she had—and gone back to sleep. In the morning she had looked down the basement stairs and seen the door open and the light burning. Everybody had heard her scream.

At a ten-cent store, Corn bought a first-aid tin and went back to his room and dressed his wound. It could have been a boil, or a shaving cut. After dark, he went out again, for dinner and another paper. The police were attaching great significance to the locked area door. The next afternoon, Corn checked out of his room. He spent the afternoon at a movie. He had dinner and read the papers. The police were questioning Leland Sessions again. He sat through another movie. When the St. Louis bus pulled out of the Union Bus Terminal at eleven-thirty Sunday night, Corn was on it.

Sitting in the Sixth Street bar, Corn smiled at the sheriff of Jackson County and his important clue. *I'm clean,* Corn thought. *I'm as clean as a whistle,* he told himself, and finished his beer. It was time he got settled in his new home. St. Louis was big enough to hold him for a while. He waved to the bartender and went out, and out on the blinding, sweltering sidewalk, the lucky tune popped into his head again.

He blinked at the cruel, glaring light, and whistled soundlessly under his breath. He wondered if his tune had a name. It would be nice to know. Corn had a tidy mind. Corn was thorough. Corn hated loose ends.

PART ONE

ONE

THE DETECTIVE TURNED HEAVILY AWAY from the window. He was a big man with a scarred red neck, a heavy chin, and a squint. He smelled of hair oil and he wore a broad, tooled-leather belt, studded with brass and colored stones. The armpits of his blue shirt were dark with sweat.

Beyond him, through the window, Leland Sessions had a view of a white all-night lunchroom across the street. A man in an undershirt stood in the doorway, picking his teeth. Above the lunchroom, a flickering neon sign blinked on and off in a second-story window: *Bail Bonds a Spec al y.* The windows above were dark and overhead the late night sky hung dim and heavy with the first heat of the summer.

The detective grunted, and the big belt creaked. He spat behind the radiator. Somewhere in the distance a streetcar rumbled over a crossing.

"All right, boy," he said. "Wake up."

Leland said, "I'm awake."

The detective gave him a long, irritable look.

"Then act like it," he said. "Stop giving us this crap."

Leland said, "It isn't—crap. I've told you everything in God's world I know."

"You heard me," the detective said. "I said it was crap."

Leland said nothing. Across the street, the neon sign blinked out and wearily on again. Sitting humped on the teetering, backless chair, he wet his lips and watched the sign without interest, and once more let his mind crawl incredulously back to probe the wreckage. It wasn't possible that this had happened to him. It still wasn't possible that his private uniqueness could have failed. But it was true, he told himself, as he had so many times through all the hours of questioning. He accepted everything, but he wasn't convinced. Conviction still sat stubbornly in the past, contesting any change from the neat desk, the comforting certainty of digits and decimals, the Saturday afternoons at the country-club pool, the long, casual evenings with people he had known all his life. Violence was only something in the newspapers, in the books on his night table.

Conviction had always lagged behind reality. Conviction had always withstood change until the last. It was blind to catastrophe. It censored out the unacceptable like hope distorting the future. Standing beside the hospital bed that afternoon five years ago, Leland had seen his father endure one final wrench of pain, and die. He had known the truth before any of them, before his mother, before the nurse, before the doctor. But conviction had blandly denied it all. *He's dead,* he had repeated to himself going down the stark medicinal corridor. *My father is dead.* It could have been merely hearsay. There had been no feeling in him at all until hours later. Conviction had vanished stealthily in the night, like a deserter. Leland had awakened in the morning to the truth, to the terror of loss.

This might have been that distant afternoon. In spite of everything—the avalanche of questions, the unconcealed dislike, the photographs in the papers—he felt nothing but a kind of numb anxiety. He ran a damp hand over his smooth black hair. It was true, but it couldn't be. It had happened to him, but it couldn't have.

The detective lighted a cigarette, sourly, as though it gave him no pleasure. He squinted at Leland through the curling smoke. Leland gazed back at the small, hard eyes.

"I'm awake," he said.

The detective only grunted. It was as though he had satisfied his last doubt, as though he had finally made up his mind about everything.

There had been too many detectives today, too many uniforms, too many questions. The big detective merged with the unsubstantiality of all the rest. *This is Police Headquarters,* Leland told himself with disbelief. He had never even been arrested for speeding. *I'm at Police Headquarters,* he thought. He stared for verification at the dusty trophies on exhibit in the corner cabinet: the railroad spike pounded into a blade, the massive frontier revolver, the deceptively domestic ice pick. And on the desk, ready to take its place with the others, was the pair of shears that were still clotted with the blood of Louise Heim. But he was here by accident, like somebody who had wandered into the wrong room and had been momentarily mistaken for somebody else. He couldn't help but feel that presently someone would appear and explain everything. There had always been someone before. There had always been help, if he needed it.

Innocence had handicapped him. He had been prepared to help, to answer the expected questions, to tell the little he knew. He had, in fact, been the one to take charge, to do what had to be done. Sophie had stood moaning in the kitchen. His mother hadn't looked. She hadn't even listened. She had covered her ears and fled. He was the one who had gone to the telephone. He was the one who had called the police and waited at the door, and led them down the stairs. He had watched them pick up the handkerchief that Aunt Belle had given him for Christmas—and even then he had felt nothing but simple astonishment. He had even— But reality had ended there in the little white-washed room at seven o'clock yesterday morning. It had melted slowly away among the uniforms and the revolvers, the notebooks and the cameras, among the detectives, the technicians, the deputy sheriffs, the coroner, the reporters, and the photographers. Someone had said,

"Thank you, Mr. Sessions. You've been very helpful. But there are still a few questions. Suppose we adjourn to . . ."

Disbelief had closed in with the escort down the familiar flagstone walk, with the official car waiting at the curb, with the siren howling through the early-morning traffic. He had sat like a stranger to himself between two holstered hips, staring at one stranger's long sideburns and at the other stranger's flattened nose. No one had spoken during that quick, accomplished drive. The questions had come later, and with them the suspicion, the anger, and the endless, incredible accusation. He could only deny it, and endure.

Leland wondered if this dim, unconvincing acceptance was weakness. It was possible that strength waited on belief. He couldn't refute an accusation that he couldn't bring himself to recognize. But strength and weakness had suddenly lost all meaning. It hadn't been weakness that led him to this chair in this gritty, midnight room. It was, if anything, strength. Weakness would have saved him. A moment of weakness last Friday night, and everything would have been different. He would have been carried away beyond the reach of any possible suspicion. But he hadn't yielded. He hadn't known. Nobody could have known. But if he had. *But if,* he told himself. *If only—* He tried to stop. He tried not to think. He tried not to remember. It was no use. Altered by hindsight into nightmare, the memory came crashing through.

It struck with the faraway howl of a Burlington freight. Sprawled peacefully silent in their chairs on the Huntings' long brick terrace, with the late-evening damp creeping up from the lawn, the four of them listened to the rise and fall and fade of sound. Then it was gone, swallowed up in a tinkle of ice on glass. Jack Huntting lowered his head. He gave an indolent grunt, scratched a white flannel thigh, and smiled across at his wife.

"Sweetie?" He held out his empty glass. "Be a good girl and fix the old man a drink."

"Yes, lord," Posy said. She stood up, sweeping a cat from

her lap and her hair from her eyes, a slim, tanned girl in tartan shorts and a calico shirt. "Anybody else? Lee?"

"I'm okay," he said.

"Me, too," Tony Evans said. "As a matter of fact, I'm fine. I just had an idea. I ran into Billy Miles the other day, and—"

"That isn't an idea," Jack said. "It's a calamity."

"Who's Billy Miles?" Posy said from the table behind her chair. "Oh, I remember. He's that big, awful, red-faced letch that crashed the Easter party." She splashed whisky into a glass and reached for a pitcher of water. "And tried to drag Debbie Duncan into the caddy house."

"You can hardly blame him for that," Jack said. "I wouldn't—"

"Careful, lord," Posy said. "You want me to poison your drink?"

"Billy's all right," Leland said. "He just thinks he's still down at Missouri. He never got over that Oklahoma game and that All-Big Six and all those thousands cheering."

"Okay," Tony said. "I agree. He's a jerk. But that isn't the point. The point is, he gets around. And he was telling me about a place he'd discovered. I thought it might be fun to take a look at it."

"You mean tonight?" Jack said. "What's the matter— aren't you getting enough to drink here?" He took his replenished glass from his wife. "Thanks, pie."

"Umm," Posy said. She sank back into her chair. "What kind of a place, Tony?"

"Just a juke joint," Tony said. "A nice one, though. They call it Feeney's or Foley's or something like that. It's over around the Plaza somewhere."

"I can hardly wait," Leland said.

"I know," Tony said. "However." He grinned. "It seems they've got a special attraction. There's a waitress there with something that you've got to see to believe. She makes Linda Darnell look flat-chested. Or so Billy said."

"Oh?" Jack said.

Posy looked at Tony and shook her head. "I wondered

what you meant by nice," she said. "I should have known."

"Well," Jack said. "If you're sure they've got a juke box. You know how I am about music. I can't get enough of it." He took a swallow of his drink. "How about you, Lee?"

"I'm the same way," Leland said. "I love good music. But not tonight. I've got to get up in the morning. I've got to work."

"What the hell," Tony said. "So do I. So does Jack."

"Don't forget me," Posy said. "I'm the one that gets Jack up. Or are you trying to include me out of this?"

"Of course not," Jack said. "Experience is the greatest of teachers. It'll do you good."

"We're all going," Tony said. "Look, Lee. All I'm suggesting is one quick drink and a look around. Then we'll blow. It can't be more than about eleven-thirty yet. You'll be home by one at the latest."

"Haw!" Leland said.

"Come on," Jack said. "Don't be like that. You remind me of my conscience."

"That ugly, wizened-up little thing?" Leland said. "God forbid." He lighted a cigarette. "But no kidding—I really can't. You know that."

"There's no such word as 'can't,'" Jack said. "We learned that in the First Form."

"Shall I twist his wrist?" Posy said.

"I wish you would," Leland said. "I'd love it. But even so—" He reached for his drink and held it up to the light. "As a matter of fact, I've got to shove off as soon as I finish this. Saturday is a tough day for me. I've got to be bright-eyed and able."

"That's the trouble with Lee," Tony said. "He's got ambition. I've seen it coming on for months. The song has gone out of his heart. He wants to get ahead—like his boss. He wants to be another Carl Upjohn."

"Exactly," Jack said. "It's an awful thing to say, but I'm afraid you're right. They're two of a kind."

"He's my ideal," Leland said. "I thought you knew that."

"I know Mr. Upjohn," Posy said. "And that's quite

enough." She giggled. "He looks like an adding machine."

"He acts like one, too," Leland said. "Especially on Saturday morning. But he's really not so bad. I mean, to work for. He's old and sour and he likes to breathe down your neck, but he's fair. He always has been with me, anyway. Of course, he doesn't know the kind of company I keep." He swallowed the last of his drink, and stood up. "Well, so long, pleasure-lovers. Have a good time. I'll see you at the Club around noon, Jack. Tony?"

"By all means," Tony said. "We'll give you a full report."

"Poor Lee," Posy said.

"So long," Jack said. "I admire you, but you're making a big mistake."

"I know," Leland said.

Well, he knew now. Reason was as blind as folly, and he had. Slumped on the back-breaking backless chair, with the knife of memory twisting and turning, he knew he had never made a bigger one. Or so many. Chance and choice had intervened at almost every step that night. And at every chance he had made a choice that had brought him closer to this. For once his mother had already gone up to her room. For once she hadn't heard him pass her door. For once he had escaped the usual home-coming ordeal of affection and complaint. For once his carefully calculated drinks had left him wide-awake. And for once, instead of searching for sleep, he had turned on the bedside light and read. He had turned it off at two.

It had all come out, dreamily damning—later in the morning, in the afternoon, last night. First, the drinks. Then the cautious passage to his room. And finally, the book.

"You say you were reading?"

"Yes."

"In your room?"

"Yes."

"Which overlooks the back yard—the garden?"

"Yes."

"The same as her room?"

"Yes. Only—well, not exactly. I mean, my room is on the second floor and more to the south. The room Louise—"

"Louise? Oh. You mean Miss Heim. That's what you called her, eh? Louise. It's a pretty name."

"She was the maid. You usually call a maid by her first name. You know that."

"Uh huh. Sure. Especially when you're screwing her every night. But go on, son. You were describing her room. It must have been pretty comfortable. Which reminds me —the way those bedsprings were oiled. That was mighty clever. You thought of everything, didn't you, son? Or almost. There were a few odds and ends. Like the body—and, of course, your handkerchief. That's what puzzles me. How you happened to forget that. Unless it just happened to slip your mind in all the excitement. Was that it, son?"

"I've told you about that. I've told you everything I know. It's my handkerchief—I never said it wasn't. I told you it was mine the minute I saw it. But I didn't leave it there. I haven't been in that room a half a dozen times in my life—not since I was a boy. I don't know how it got there. I swear I don't. I don't know anything but what I've already told you."

"You were just sitting up there in your room—reading?"

"Yes."

"At two o'clock in the morning."

"Yes—until about then. I don't remember exactly."

"And all the windows were wide open?"

"Yes."

"But you didn't hear a thing?"

"No. I told you I was reading. I guess I was—well, absorbed. It was an exciting book."

"Reading. While somebody was being murdered in your own house. While a girl was screaming for help right outside your window. But you were too busy reading to notice. You were absorbed. You didn't hear a thing. You expect me to believe that?"

"No. I mean, yes. I can't explain it. But it's the truth. I

didn't hear a . . ."

Everyone had faintly and derisively smiled.

He had had only four hours of sleep when Sophie discovered the body, and screamed. He had heard that. He could still hear those choking screams, and the sound of her pounding up the stairs from the kitchen. The memory arrested weariness for an instant. It was as vivid as actuality. But for an instant only. He couldn't hold his mind on anything now. He was too tired, too bewildered, too close to fear. *I've got to think,* he told himself. *There must be some way.* His mind wandered off in all directions, like spilled water.

Silence sat uneasily beyond the open window. He shifted his long, tired body warily on the uncertain chair. An ache twisted up and down his back. He wondered what time it was. He wondered what had become of the other detective. He remembered him standing by the cabinet, filing his nails. And then, abruptly, he was gone. He wondered why and where. He turned his head. The big detective was leaning against the desk. His cigarette hung from a corner of his mouth and he was squinting at Leland with a kind of patient contempt.

Leland said, "Could you give me a cigarette?" He had discarded his empty package at noon. But pride had held out until now.

"I'm fresh out," the detective said.

"Oh," Leland said. "Well—could I send out for some?"

"I don't know how," the detective said. He looked at him sharply. "Unless you mean me. You ain't asking me to run your errands, boy?"

"No," Leland said. "I mean—" He didn't really know what he meant. "I just thought—"

"Think again," the detective said. His face tightened as though he had stood all he could.

"I didn't mean you," Leland said.

The detective pushed himself away from the desk. "I know your trouble, boy. The trouble with you is you got a guilty conscience." His hand went up threateningly.

He said, "Ain't that right, boy? Ain't that why you got to smoke so much?"

Leland stiffened on the chair. He thought he was going to be struck. He said, "You—"

The door opened and the other detective came in. He was a thin, middle-aged man with a lodge button in the lapel of his gray mohair coat. He had a mild, clerical air and glassy false teeth and he was carrying three glasses of water.

"Trouble?" he said.

The big detective shrugged. "He hurts," he said. "His conscience bothers him."

"I can imagine," the thin detective said. He gave Leland a sympathetic smile and ranged the glasses on the desk. Two of them were full to the brim and sparkling with ice. There was no ice in the third glass and it contained a scant inch of water. He picked up the third glass and handed it to Leland. "I thought you might be thirsty, son. I know I am. A man needs a lot of water on a night like this."

Leland looked at him. But he took the water. "Thanks," he said.

"Don't mention it," the thin detective said.

The other glasses beaded like juleps on the desk. The big detective picked one up, without interest. He put it down again. "Guess what?" he said. "Now he wants me to run errands for him."

"Really?" the thin detective said. He looked at Leland curiously. "What's got into you, son?"

Leland said nothing.

"He's getting too smart for his britches," the big detective said. "First he sends you for water. Then he wants me to run down the street and fetch him some cigarettes."

"You're a puzzle to me, son," the thin detective said. He shook his head, like an aggrieved parent.

The big detective dropped the remains of his cigarette onto the floor. He stepped on it with a kind of finality. "Next thing you know," he said, "he'll try to tell us he didn't cut that girl."

The thin detective sat carefully down in the desk chair. His face was grave. He sighed.

"I hope not, Ernie," he said. "I certainly hope you're mistaken."

"Maybe," Ernie said.

"No," the thin detective said. "I really think you've misjudged the boy. I don't think he's foolish enough to make a statement like that. Not now."

"Maybe," the big detective said. He lighted another cigarette.

"No," the other said. "Not now. Not after telling us only a few minutes ago that he had been intimate with Miss Heim for several months. I really think he's going to tell us the rest of the truth and put an end to all this unpleasantness."

Leland stopped breathing. He stared at the two alien faces. He hardly recognized them as human.

The big detective said, "He said he'd been laying her five months now." He turned his eyes suddenly on Leland. "Ain't that what you said, boy? Five months?"

Leland said, "No. I didn't say that. You know damn well I didn't. I never said—"

The thin detective said, "He's right, Ernie. He didn't say five months. I remember now. He said since March. That's only about four. We want to be fair about this."

Somewhere an automobile changed gear. The sound rose and fell and died away in the distance.

Leland said, "What are you trying to do? You can't put words in my mouth. I've told you a hundred times I—"

Neither of them looked at him. He might not have been there at all. The two detectives might have been alone in the room.

The thin detective ran his tongue over his lips, thoughtfully. There was a copy of the *Saturday Evening Post* on the desk. The big detective picked it up. With his cigarette between his lips and his head tilted back to avoid the smoke, he began to roll the magazine into a long, tight cylinder.

"You'd better close the window," the thin detective said. "There aren't many people on the street this time of night. Still—" He smiled. "And you might just drop the blind while you're at it."

The big detective gave the magazine a final twist.

"Just between us girls," he said, and laughed abruptly. The thin detective sighed.

Leland said, "What—what is this?"

The big detective walked around the desk and over to the window. The magazine was clamped securely under his arm. The window came grinding down. He reached for the cord of the Venetian blind.

Leland said, "What are you going to do? You're not—" And then he knew. Fear struck him like a cramp. It tore him up from his chair. He lunged for the door.

Behind him the Venetian blind came down with a clatter. The big detective said, "Get away from that door, boy."

"Never mind, Ernie," the thin detective said. "He isn't going anywhere. I believe I locked the door."

It was true. The handle was as rigid as rock. Leland turned and faced them, and it was real now. This was reality. But it wasn't what he had expected. Belief wasn't strength. It wasn't even courage. It was panic.

"Wait," he said. "Listen. Listen to me. I swear—"

"Come here, boy," the big detective said.

TWO

Mrs. Roach opened the shade a cautious crack. She peered surreptitiously out. But her stealth was merely habit. She wasn't spying this time. She only wanted to set her watch. Two children raced around and around the lamp post at the corner, a bus wallowed away from the curb, a man in wilted seersucker loitered under the awning of the lingerie shop, and the white June sun blazed down like a shower of sparks. The clock in the jeweler's window said one-thirty.

Mrs. Roach let the shade drop and moved back into the twilight of her cluttered third-floor room. It was almost time to go. The thought brought a flush to her dry gray cheeks. From the moment the announcement had appeared in the paper, Mrs. Roach had been counting the hours. "Wild horses couldn't keep me away," she said to the photograph of Mr. Roach in its cardboard frame on the bureau. "I wouldn't miss it for the world," she said, as though that mild enduring face were still alive, as though after all these years he could still listen, and agree. But it was almost time. She began to hurry, smoothing the brown-and-green silk over the bony hips, pinning the pink cameo brooch at the sagging throat, rubbing the black, sensible shoes with a bit of cloth. It wasn't really late. She had comfortably more than an hour. But Mrs. Roach was too experienced to dawdle. She knew what to expect after four days of headlines and two full pages of pictures. The crowd, she thought with relish, might even be a record.

Mrs. Roach dampened the cloth with the tip of her tongue and wondered when she had been so excited over a funeral. Thirteen years had made her a connoisseur. She had begun to pick and choose. Not that she ever missed an important service. But every year there were more and more to which only duty called her. She no longer fully responded to anything but wealth or position or violence. Mrs. Roach creaked to her feet and hung the shoe cloth on its hook. Louise Heim was only a servant, but death had doubly redeemed her. Mrs. Roach knew the Sessions family only too well. In her seventeen years behind the notions counter at Emery-Bird-Thayer & Co., she had waited on Mrs. Sessions often enough to read her high-and-mighty character like a book. And the funeral of Arthur Sessions was one she would always remember. The services had been private. They hadn't let her in. But now— She smiled. It had seemed like fate when she opened the paper on Saturday evening and saw their faces—the haughty mother and her suspiciously handsome son—and read their shameful evasions. Mrs. Roach knew the truth when she saw it. Leland Sessions had been questioned for twenty consecutive hours by the police, released, and then questioned again. Where there was smoke, Mrs. Roach thought, there was bound to be fire.

Mrs. Roach opened the closet door and felt in the dark for her black straw hat. It was almost new. She had worn it for the first time at old Judge Benton's funeral in April. Blowing the dust from the cockade of roses and violets, she asked herself what she would ever have done if she hadn't discovered the comfort of a well-ordered funeral after Mr. Roach passed away. Not everybody, of course, agreed. She remembered the time she had tried to explain it to Mrs. Andersen. "I don't understand the attitude of some people," she had said. "Why, a nice, artistic service isn't depressing at all. It's a thing of beauty." But Mrs. Ander-

sen had only shaken her head. "They give me the creeps,"
she said. *The creeps,* Mrs. Roach thought, setting her hat
firmly on her dry gray head. *The creeps,* she thought with
a flutter of indignation. A lovely service was a refreshment.
It was like a tonic. She had noticed often enough the mirac-
ulous effect that a nice funeral always had on the recurring
pain in her back. *The creeps,* she thought, and couldn't
help the thin, vindictive smile that touched her lips. Mrs.
Andersen was always the first to ask who the important
guests had been.

Mrs. Roach picked up her pocketbook and took a last
look around the room: the ecru lace dresser scarf, the
beaded shade on the lamp, the India print bedspread, the
warm shawl folded over the back of the mechanical rocker,
the medicine bottles on the washstand shelf. Everything
was in its place. She opened the door and stepped into the
narrow, uncarpeted hall. The light from the unshaded
window made her blink. A dog had replaced the man
under the lingerie shop awning. The jeweler's clock said
one fifty-five. She hurried down the stairs, past the rubber
plant on the second-floor landing, past the peeling, dis-
colored walls, past Mrs. Andersen's closed door. On the
way to the streetcar stop on the corner, Mrs. Roach found
herself thinking again of Louise Heim. *That poor girl,* she
thought, *that poor, innocent, deceived child.* It was too
horrible, and she could hardly wait to be in her place, shar-
ing in the dignified sorrow. *Men,* she murmured under her
breath, and was stirred by the sound of the word. They
only wanted one thing. *Not Mr. Roach, of course,* she told
herself quickly, *not Mr. Roach.* He had never given her a
minute's anxiety, and he had passed to his reward as peacefully and gently as he had lived. She had accepted every
word he said on politics and wild-life conservation. *No,*
she thought, *not Mr. Roach.* The other kind. Strong young
men like— Mrs. Roach broke into a trot. A streetcar was
coming. She wouldn't have to wait. It was a good sign, an
omen. It meant that this was one of her days. It was a
promise that she would be in time to get her favorite place,

well to the front and a little to the right, with a view of the private room where the family would sit.

Mrs. Roach deposited her token and caught her breath. "That poor, innocent child," she thought, and wasn't aware that she had spoken the words aloud until a rough young man across the aisle glanced up and smirked. *Men*, she thought, and looked deliberately straight ahead at the black, revolting stain of sweat on the back of the motorman's shirt. Mrs. Roach had read every word that every paper had printed about the murder, and she knew who the murderer was. She knew who had murdered Louise Heim, and why. She knew it as well as she knew that the doctors were wrong, that there *was* a lump in her left breast, and that it was cancer. Mrs. Roach knew the vileness of men when they had gratified their animal passions. She had heard Mr. and Mrs. Cortina at night in their room next door, and she had seen Mr. Cortina in the hall. She had recognized the evidence of his great thighs, his massive, muscled arms. Leland Sessions was thinner than Mr. Cortina, but he was marked by the same taint. It was there to be seen in his picture. Even Mrs. Andersen admitted that he looked like a killer. The motorman clanged his bell. A boy on a bicycle weaved languidly out of the way. Mrs. Roach roused herself from reflection. Her stop was approaching. She clutched her pocketbook under her arm and reeled down the aisle toward pleasure.

The Horace B. Duncan Funeral Home was just around the corner. As it came into view, Mrs. Roach quickened her pace. She wasn't a moment too soon. There were already people drifting up the walk, and the steps were almost crowded. Mrs. Roach recognized one of the directors on the broad, pillared porch, and the attendant at the door. But she hadn't been prepared for the others—the two policemen at the foot of the steps, the three men who could only be detectives, the young man with the camera. A sudden thrill of excitement carried her breathlessly up the steps and past the familiar director. She returned his correct smile, but she avoided the glances of the others.

One of the detectives, the one with the peculiar eyes, was as powerful as Mr. Cortina.

Inside, in the foyer, everything was also somehow different. There was, as usual, the heavy breath of flowers, the guarded light, the rich illusion of splendor. But there was something else. Mrs. Roach surprised a young woman in a shameless grin. Behind her, somebody snickered. There were even people here and there who couldn't be bothered to whisper. Mrs. Roach set her face. She, at least, had respect. She moved gauntly down between the pews, past the roped-off reserved sections, and found the place she wanted. The organ throbbed a soothing chord. She was just in time. Mrs. Roach adjusted her skirt and took out her handkerchief, and covertly craned her neck. The chapel was almost full. Late arrivals were crowding in from the foyer. Most of them, she noticed with satisfaction, would have to stand. A young man with a small mustache lounged in a corner with a pad of paper and a pencil. While she watched, he stared down the aisle and scribbled a lazy note. Mrs. Roach was used to reporters. They were always at the better services. One had once sat beside her and read a magazine. Mrs. Roach sighed, studying the faces —but it was always a mixed crowd at funerals of this sort.

The organ trembled on a long note, and Mrs. Roach turned back. Hidden by a screen of flowers, a tenor began to sing. Mrs. Roach touched her handkerchief to her eyes. The hymn was her favorite.

"Let there be no moaning at the bar,
When I put out to sea . . ."

The flowers on the altar were a trifle disappointing. She had expected more. The banked plants and blooms actually thinned out a few feet beyond the coffin. *Poor child,* she thought, peering between the heads of the man and the woman in the pew in front. *Friendless,* she thought, *poor, friendless waif.* One would think that a family like the Sessionses, with their wealth and their position—and their guilt—would have the decency to properly honor the child's last resting place.

There was a sudden attentive stir. Mrs. Roach raised her eyes. The minister was standing before them now, silent in his black vestments, slightly bowed. He stood at the lectern, an old man with a high forehead and a mane of silvery hair, adjusting the tiny beam of the reading lamp. He softly cleared his throat. Mrs. Roach nodded, with approval. He was the rector of one of the largest churches. *Still,* she thought, *those flowers.* The minister gazed into space. It was like a signal. The music dissolved into silence.

The minister closed his eyes: "I am the resurrection and the life, saith the Lord: he that believeth in me, though he were dead, yet shall he live: and whosoever liveth and believeth in me, shall never die . . ."

Mrs. Roach thought of poor Louise Heim knowing peace at last, and looked at the coffin. She had hoped the lid would be left open. She would have liked a glimpse of the poor little child.

"We brought nothing into this world, and it is certain we can carry nothing out. The Lord gave, and the Lord hath taken away; blessed be the name of the Lord . . ."

The poor child, Mrs. Roach thought again, and she had never felt such sympathy before. Louise Heim had lived so briefly, and she had known nothing but the proof of man's vileness, his animal appetite. Mrs. Roach swallowed. Mr. Cortina strode heavily across her mind.

"For man walketh in the vain shadow, and disquieteth himself in vain: he heapeth up riches, and cannot tell who shall gather them. Glory be to the Father, and to the Son: and to the Holy Ghost . . ."

Riches, Mrs. Roach thought. She cautiously turned her head. Now that the aisles were clear, she had a view of the inner chapel. She peered obliquely into the shadows. Across the plain of lowered heads she could just make out a pale cheek, a sweep of graying hair, the dipping brim of a dark-blue hat. *Look at her,* she thought, *just look at her.* But it wasn't enough. It wasn't the mother she wanted. Mrs. Roach strained her eyes at the dusk—and caught her breath. A dark trouser leg, a patch of dark sock, and the heel of a black shoe extended beyond a corner of the dark, paneled wall. *That's him,* she thought, with certainty and disappointment. But his face—she had to see his face. She had to see that mocking smile, those vicious, heartless eyes.

"Lord, thou has been our refuge: from one generation to another. Before the mountains were brought forth, or ever the earth and the world were made: thou art God from everlasting, and world without end. Thou turnest man to destruction: again thou sayest, Come again, ye children of men . . ."

The words took root in Mrs. Roach's mind. *Destruction,* she thought, as she secretly strained and watched, and the usual word had never before held such a wealth of meaning. Never before had its application been so plain. *Destruction,* she thought with a shiver, and prayed for something more than a leg, an ankle, and a foot.

"For we consume away in thy displeasure: and are afraid at thy wrathful indignation. Thou hast set our misdeeds before thee: our secret sins in the light of thy countenance. For when thou art angry all our days are gone: we bring our years to an end, as it were a tale that is told . . ."

Mrs. Roach was suddenly aware that the Sessions family was not alone in the private room. There was another woman there. Her face was hidden. She was only a swell of breast and shoulder. Mrs. Roach stared, and wondered. Could it be— But it couldn't. Little Louise was an orphan. The newspapers, she remembered, had made something of a point of that. But who, she thought, and then, with a thrill, she knew. It was the cook. It could only be the cook. It was Mrs. Binder. It was the woman who had found the body of the poor, dead child. Mrs. Roach felt a tremor of horror and delight.

"For since by man came death, by man came also the resurrection of the dead. For as in Adam all die, so even in Christ shall all be made alive. But every man in his own order: Christ, the firstfruits; afterward they that are

Christ's at His coming. Then cometh the end, when he shall have delivered up the kingdom of God, even the Father: when he shall have put down all rule and all authority and power. For He must reign, till He hast put all enemies under His feet. The last enemy that shall be destroyed is death . . ."

Sitting there in all their wealth and pride, Mrs. Roach thought, *sitting there with blood on their hands.* She strained her eyes. She had to see. *Rich libertines,* she thought, rolling the vaguely profane word on her tongue. She even included the cook. *Rich—* Her throat went tight. It was all she could do not to gasp. The wide-brimmed hat had moved. Mrs. Roach stared into the face of the murderer, and the murderer stared at her. For a moment, she could only stare. Then she narrowed her eyes and slowly released her practiced, venomous smile. It struck. She saw it strike. She saw the start as the poison struck. She saw his flush of guilt and dismay. Now he knew. Mrs. Roach nodded her head and smiled again. Now he knew what decent people thought. The hatbrim moved once more. It dropped like a curtain across the dark head, the dark eyes, the dark, shaven jaw. Mrs. Roach lowered her head and smiled a smile that only she could see. He had read her knowledge. He knew.

"Behold!" Mrs. Roach almost started. It was like a confirmation. The gently exultant voice went on: "I show you a mystery: We shall not all sleep, but we shall all be changed, in a moment, in the twinkling of an eye, at the last trump; for the trumpet shall sound, and the dead shall be raised incorruptible, and we shall all be changed . . ."

Mrs. Roach fixed her gaze on the sweet old face.

THREE

M̲r̲. U̲p̲j̲o̲h̲n̲ d̲r̲o̲v̲e̲ h̲i̲m̲s̲e̲l̲f̲ a̲c̲r̲o̲s̲s̲ t̲h̲e̲ s̲i̲d̲e̲w̲a̲l̲k̲ and up the wide, shallow steps of the Cattlemen's Bank & Trust Company. Halfway up the steps, his chest tightened and his heart began its familiar, breathless flutter. It made him wince, but he didn't pause. He climbed briskly on—an angular man with a sun-lamp tan and his hair cut short to disguise the dangerous glitter of gray. His heart was the least of his worries. He almost dared it to stop and almost hoped it would. Anything would be better than this. His mind was made up, but his conscience still held out. He ached with the thought of what he had to do.

The chairman of the board had said nothing, but Mr. Upjohn was alert to a hint and he knew the value of the anticipated wish. He had climbed to success by knowing the mind of the man just ahead of him. Every step of his lonely way had sharpened his eye and his instinct. Mr. Upjohn was the only officer of the bank who hadn't been to college. *I haven't any choice,* he thought, and tried to shoulder doubt away as he had old Osborne and Major Dupree and Richard Henry Garretson of the Harvard Business School. Thirty years of faithful service had given Mr. Upjohn a ruthless respect for expediency. It was impossible to exaggerate the significance of the chairman's remark only last winter about the unusual promise shown by several of the younger men. He hadn't, of course, men-

51

tioned any names. But that was beside the point. Mr. Upjohn would be sixty-three in September.

"Good morning, Mr. Upjohn." It was the doorman. He touched his cap and flung open the big barred door. "It looks like we're in for another scorcher, don't it?" The sweat was already dark on his tan uniform shirt.

Mr. Upjohn gazed at the sweated shirt and became for the first time aware of the heat. The June sun streamed down between the marble columns. It pressed like a hand on his neck.

"Good morning, Homer," he said, and hesitated, weighing the risk. But only the younger officers could afford to feel the heat. Mr. Upjohn was too vulnerable. He added, "Yes. It is—warm." He walked briskly on.

An assistant vice-president nodded a mild good morning from a desk beside the marble counter. An early customer gave him an idle stare. A bookkeeper stepped elaborately aside, and improvised an elaborate smile.

"Good morning," Mr. Upjohn said, and turned his withdrawn face from side to side. "Good morning."

Mr. Upjohn wondered if his torment could be seen. He straightened his shoulders and hardened his jaw. He tried to harden his heart. *I'm right,* he thought. *I am only doing what is right.* He told himself: *It's for his own good.* But it was no use. Doubt kept pace with him all the way down the vaulted marble aisle. It was only nine o'clock, but his bones were already limp with fatigue. He had scarcely slept at all last night. Lying in his stifling bed in his corner suite at the Kansas City Club, he had listened to the fading murmur of traffic from the streets nine stories below, and miserably marshaled his reasons. Nothing could hold out against the wisdom of thirty years. He had won every skirmish. He had turned every attack into a rout. But every victory had ended in another defeat.

Behind their bars, the tellers stiffened. Their smiles flashed on like electric lights. For a moment Mr. Upjohn's spirits lifted. His head bobbed gravely up and down. This was what he had worked for. It was for this that he had given his life. The suite at the club and the custom-made clothes were wholly incidental. For a dozen steps he could almost believe that he had somehow finally won. For a moment, reason almost prevailed. But only for a moment. The anxious smile on the new face in U-W abruptly destroyed it all. Until today, Mr. Upjohn had been able to tell himself that the change was merely temporary.

"Good morning, Mr. Upjohn."

This time it was a guard. Mr. Upjohn nodded, but he had no idea what the man had said. He couldn't be sure that the man had even spoken. All Mr. Upjohn could hear was the sound of his own voice as he had stood five years before in the shaded hospital room, repeating his promise to his old friend, the only real friend that he had ever had.

"Like I told the wife this morning," the guard said. "Anybody would think this was August instead of only June."

Mr. Upjohn stared at him. His own voice thundered in his head: "Forget about Lee. You know perfectly well I settled that long ago. The place is waiting for him. If he likes, he can start the day after graduation. And with his record, he'll probably put us both in the shade. The only thing you have to think about is getting well in time for some duck-hunting next month."

The guard said, "Ninety-three in the shade. I just looked."

"Ummm," Mr. Upjohn said, and pulled open the gate in the counter.

There had been no gunning that fall at Arthur Sessions's shack in Cass County. Arthur had lingered, recognizing no one those last few days, until the season was almost gone. Mr. Upjohn had never touched his shotgun again. Gunning meant Arthur Sessions. Gunning meant that particular shack. There was no substitute for either. Arthur Sessions had been more than a friend. Mr. Upjohn owed him almost everything, including his career. The old Sessions Grain Company account had really given him his start. Mr. Upjohn clutched the knob of his office door. He stared at the gilded legend: *Carl A. Upjohn, Second Vice-President.* He turned his eyes away. It might have been a reproach. *But I'm right,* he thought. *I'm only doing what is right. Arthur would understand. Arthur would be the first to understand. Arthur would know that I'm only thinking of Lee. It wouldn't be fair to the boy.* A telephone uttered an urgent cry in the chairman's office next door.

Mr. Upjohn gave the knob a frantic wrench. *If only the police would do something,* he thought. *Lee didn't do it. Everybody knows he didn't do it. But they've had almost two weeks. What do we pay them for? They can't believe he—* He wondered suddenly if it was a question of politics. Maybe somebody was being protected. But it was impossible to know. Mr. Upjohn had limited his political activities to the municipality of the bank. He tottered through the door.

Miss Franklin was bending over his desk, arranging a spray of lilacs in a vase. She sprang erect, as though he had surprised her rifling a drawer.

"Oh," she said, and a smile jerked into place on her face. "Good morning, Mr. Upjohn."

"Good morning, Miss Franklin."

Mr. Upjohn hung his straw hat on the rack in the corner. As always, the dim, featureless face of the chairman of the board eyed him from the elegantly framed photograph of the Fiftieth Anniversary Dinner of the Cattlemen's Bank & Trust Company. His own unrecognizable face peered at him from the foot of the speakers' table. He had been an assistant vice-president in the credit department then. The chairman of the board had complimented him later on his brief talk on Responsibility. *Responsibility,* Mr. Upjohn thought. He hadn't even glimpsed responsibility in those days. He turned wearily away.

Miss Franklin said, "Oh, Mr. Upjohn. That Mr. Bell at Mid-West Tile called a few minutes ago. I—"

Mr. Upjohn made a vague, unhappy gesture.

"All right," he said. "Will you leave a memorandum for me."

"It's on your desk now, Mr. Upjohn," she said.

"Good," he said. "Thank you."

He smiled at her with a kind of curiosity. It was as though he were seeing her for the first time in months. It occurred to him that he wasn't even sure of her first name. *Would she be hurt,* he asked himself, *if she knew I'd forgotten her name?* The deep ache of personal doubt gave him a brief, unhappy sympathy for everyone. He wondered if his curt reply had alarmed the guard, if the tellers had read blame or approval in his greetings. For a moment Mr. Upjohn saw fear and worry everywhere.

Miss Franklin said, "Was there anything else, Mr. Upjohn?"

"No, I think not," he said, and suddenly remembered her name. It jumped into his mind with a forgotten incident of six weeks ago. Returning from lunch that day, he had found himself walking behind a group of typists from the trust department. He hadn't meant to listen. But her name had arrested him: Angie Franklin. He remembered the ripple of giggles. And then: "So now she's gunning for Miss Prather's job. She's going to end up as private secretary to the president. Or bust." Angie Franklin, he thought, and tried to relate the familiar, seething fever of ambition to that dry, anonymous face.

Mr. Upjohn let himself down in his chair.

He said, "Oh, Miss Franklin."

"Yes, Mr. Upjohn?"

His sympathy petered abruptly out. It left him hollow. For a moment, he hadn't the strength to speak. He sat empty and alone, indifferent to everybody: the guards, the tellers, Miss Franklin, Leland Sessions, the chairman of the board—all of them. He needed all his sympathy for himself.

Miss Franklin stood at the door, with a kind of aggressive patience.

He said, heavily, "I'm expecting Mr. Sessions."

The curiosity he had felt a moment before might have been that of another man. He lacked the interest now even to raise his eyes to detect whatever surprise might have come into his secretary's face.

"He should be here in a very few minutes. Show him in at once."

"Yes, Mr. Upjohn."

He added, "I won't be able to see anyone else for at least an hour." *An hour,* he thought. He ran his hands slowly down the arms of his chair. In an hour it would be all over.

"Yes, Mr. Upjohn."

As she left, he glanced up. He looked at the thin, maidenly hips and the neat bun of dead-brown hair. Ambition had kept Mr. Upjohn a bachelor. With distaste, he watched the ambitious spinster close the door.

In an hour, Mr. Upjohn thought. *I haven't really any choice,* he told himself. *If it weren't I, it would be somebody else.* He closed his eyes against the sudden stab of doubt. *It might not even take an hour,* he thought. *There isn't really much to say. Unless—* He tried to block the pain with a picture of Albert Bell and the tangled finances of the Mid-West Tile Company. Even the idea of another interview with Bell was fantastic. The situation was hopeless. At best, another loan could only postpone the collapse. He thought: *I told him that last week.* But his conscience wouldn't let him look ahead.

Mr. Upjohn opened his eyes. And it was like a blow. His eyes opened on the photograph on the wall between the windows. He couldn't read the faded inscription in Arthur Sessions's feathery hand, but he knew it by heart. And, in spite of himself, he remembered the occasion. He saw the room lighted against the early December night, the fire snapping on the hearth, and the three of them smiling over their festive Tom and Jerrys. The gift wrapping crackled again as he worked the ribbon off the corner of the package. He heard Arthur clear his throat. He heard him say; "Madge says only a Rudolph Valentino would give somebody a picture of himself. But . . ." Mr. Upjohn deafened himself to the rest of the warm, stumbling sincerity. He tried to take comfort in the thought that Madge Sessions had never really liked him. She had, he knew, never really forgiven him for being the son of a railroad conductor. But it was to Arthur that he had made his promise.

The argument sawed back and forth in Mr. Upjohn's mind, brutal and heartless and without end. Somewhere in the bank a bell clanged. Somewhere a door slammed. Somewhere a battery of adding machines opened a wild barrage. Beyond the windows, a mutter of voices passed along the street. Somebody somewhere was whistling as tunelessly as a bird. A brake shrieked, and a horn blew and blew. Feet scraped on the sidewalk and a newsboy shouted his fabricated excitement. The hot smell of traffic pressed through the windows. Mr Upjohn sat rigid in his chair, oblivious to it all. *Arthur would know,* he told himself again. *I know he would understand. Any businessman would.* The dead eyes in the photograph were noncommittal behind the rimless glasses. The faint smile on the dead mouth only spoke of friendship.

Mr. Upjohn turned his gaze to the lilacs. It was safer. After all, he told himself, *I do have a responsibility to the bank. A bank is a public institution. It is founded on public trust. On confidence.* And it took so little these days to precipitate the most disastrous complications. Mr. Upjohn thought of Aaron Silberman. The mere appointment of Silberman to the board a year ago had irretrievably lost the valuable Müller Foundry account. The vote had been unanimous, but all that was remembered now was that Mr. Upjohn had been the first to propose Silberman's name.

Mr. Upjohn told himself that it wasn't as if the severance would be permanent. In a few months the whole distressing affair would be forgotten. The police were bound to find the right man eventually. He wondered if his problem would have been easier if his old friend's son had actually— But that was ridiculous. Even the papers had stopped hinting after the first few days. But the truth altered nothing. *In six months,* he told himself. *Or a year at the most. Then he'll be back on the job.* He thought with satisfaction: *A better job. A much better job.* He gave himself a cheerful picture of the two of them a year from now, laughing about it all over lunch. *It's really for his own good,* he told himself. *It wouldn't be fair to let him come back next week and work in that public room all day. I wouldn't have the heart.*

Mr. Upjohn picked up the Bell memorandum, and put it down. He found it necessary to clear his throat. *If he really needed the job,* he told himself. *It might be different if he had to have the job. But he doesn't.* He wondered suddenly if Leland Sessions had ever fully realized what his father's old friend had done for him. Lee was a smart boy. His grasp of the whole theory of credit was truly remarkable. But that didn't mean that a few words by the right man in the right place hadn't helped. With the beginning of annoyance, Mr. Upjohn thought: *It probably never entered his head.* His mind took a bound: *I'll wager he'll jump at the chance to take a real vacation.* A memory of his own uneasy holidays floated distantly through his head. He thought: *He could run down to Mexico for the summer. In the fall he could go back East and see a few shows.* Mr. Upjohn had never been to Mexico. He had spent three days in New York in 1931, winding up the reorganization of the Gypsy Queen Milling Company. He thought, with envy and exasperation: *He'll have the time of his life. Absolutely,* he told himself. *The time—* He looked at his watch. It was nine thirty-two.

Mr. Upjohn frowned. *He ought to be here by now,* he thought. He gave a twitch of annoyance. He thought: *He could at least be punctual. Especially at a time like this.* He picked up the Bell memorandum again and glared at the evidence of Albert Bell's stupidity. *Bert Bell,* he thought. Young Bell was thirty years old, and active in the Friends of Art. There was another boy who had never known what it was to shift for himself. Mr. Upjohn asked himself what E. K. Bell would think if he were alive today to observe his son's stewardship of the business that he had founded. The answer gave him an instant of bitter satisfaction. He let the memorandum drop. He took a deep breath and waited.

I could have told him over the telephone, he thought. *I could have called him up, or written. But I wanted to do the right thing. I'm willing to take the time to explain. He knows my schedule. He knows what an hour of my time is worth. He might at least have the courtesy to be punctual.* He ran his hands up and down the arms of his chair, and felt annoyance sharpen. He looked again at his watch. It was nine thirty-five. It was an imposition. He thought: *Where is he? Doesn't he realize? Hasn't he got the common consideration?* His hands gripped the chair arms. He thought: *I distinctly said nine-thirty.*

Mr. Upjohn thrust back his chair. He pushed himself to his feet. *Why isn't he here?* he thought, and it was as though the sudden movement had shattered all his doubts. *The puppy,* he thought. *The inconsiderate puppy. After all I've done for him.* With a violence that shook him almost to nausea, he drove down the reality of his security, the shame of his ambition, and welcomed the simplicity of anger. He stood behind the desk that he had fought so hard to reach and let the saving anger rise to fury. He had to clutch the arm of the chair to keep himself erect, but the real weakness, the fatal inner weakness, was gone.

There was a knock at the door. Mr. Upjohn swung around. He tried to speak, and couldn't. His throat was too dry. He swallowed. "Come," he said. "Come in." The fury was running through his veins, and he was ready.

It was Miss Franklin.

"Mr. Sessions is here, Mr. Upjohn," she said.

She stepped back and away. Leland moved past her, with a kind of smile, into the familiar room. The door closed behind him.

"Good morning, Uncle Carl," he said. "I'm sorry if I'm

late, but Mr. Damon—" He took another step, and stopped. The remains of the smile withered on his lips. He hardly recognized the man who faced him across the desk. The mouth was the mouth of the leering old woman at the funeral. The eyes were the glazed gray eyes of the detective with the magazine twisted into a club.

"I see," Mr. Upjohn said.

It was a voice that Leland had never heard before.

FOUR

SITTING ALONE IN THE BIG DINING-ROOM with the faded portraits staring from the white paneled walls, Mrs. Sessions struggled with uneasiness. A hot gasp of breeze stirred the curtains at the open windows behind her. The candles on the table flickered. Flame danced on the polished mahogany and darted like lightning over the silver on the Sheraton sideboard. Mrs. Sessions touched her handkerchief to her upper lip, and tried to tell herself that it was the heat.

She could hear Sophie in the kitchen, rattling a pan, running water in the sink, humming something that went tonelessly on and on. Out on the lawn, the long June twilight lingered like a watcher. It was really too warm for candles. But Mrs. Sessions couldn't bring herself to have them removed. They stood for tranquillity and peace. They stood as a kind of bulwark against the outrage that was somehow symbolized tonight by the empty chair across the table. Mrs. Sessions opened the small enameled case beside her plate. She dropped a grain of saccharine into her tea, and thought: *Where is he?* The reluctant question was suddenly an admission. She added a slice of lemon and a stick of clove to her cup, and let her defenses crumble. It wasn't the heat. There was no use pretending. She wanted him, and he wasn't here. She thought: *Why doesn't he call? He could do that. He could let me know.*

She couldn't understand it. It was as though he always had before. It was as though she had always cared. Mrs. Sessions shaped her life to the vital fictions passed by her personal censor. She looked unhappily at the empty place, at the evidence she refused to understand. She couldn't understand why he wasn't there to respond to her need, to listen and reassure. She thought: *He knew I had one of my headaches. I told him so at lunch. When he mentioned that unspeakable girl. That vile, ungrateful—* But she preferred not to think about that. The world was so full of ugly things. She only yearned for happiness. Mrs. Sessions groped with her foot for the bulge of the carpet and pressed the buzzer.

Sophie came through the door from the pantry, rubbing her hands on her apron. She was short, stout, and stolid. She had on a pair of red felt slippers.

"Ma'am?" she said.

"Yes," Mrs. Sessions said, and averted her eyes from the damp hands and the slovenly feet. Sophie wasn't used to serving after all these years, but she was loyal. Mrs. Sessions hadn't the heart, or the courage, to complain. She said, "I've finished, Sophie. I don't believe I care for dessert. I'll drink my tea in the living-room."

"Yes, ma'am," Sophie said. She glanced at the empty place, at the napkin in its silver ring, at the ice melted in the water glass. "Should I leave—"

Mrs. Sessions stood up. "No," she said. "I—" She smiled. "I'm afraid I forgot to tell you, Sophie. Mr. Leland won't be home to dinner tonight."

"Yes, ma'am," Sophie said, and began to blow out the candles.

Mrs. Sessions walked slowly across the empty hall, toward the lonely, twilit living-room. She thought: *Did he tell me?* Mrs. Sessions was fifty-seven years old and her hair was white and her mouth was drawn, but she had the carriage and the figure of a woman of thirty. She had always had that, and more. It had always been, until these last few years, enough. Mrs. Sessions had never needed friends. She had been satisfied with acquaintances, and admirers. *Perhaps he did tell me,* she thought. *He could have told me and I could have forgotten.* It was quite possible. That had happened more than once. Mrs. Sessions was aware that she didn't always listen. That had once been part of her charm. Hope gave a tentative stir, and died. She wasn't seeking an explanation. It was only that he wasn't here.

Mrs. Sessions glided through the deepening dark to the sofa and the coffee table. She put down her cup and switched on a lamp; the furniture sprang into color and shape and familiarity. *I'm his mother,* she thought. *I don't understand.* She thought of Amy Bell and her sweet, handsome, devoted son. Amy and Bert were inseparable. Mrs. Sessions sighed. It was unnatural. She needed him. They needed each other. She wanted to tell him of his need. She wanted him to share the comfort of her faith, the faith that had shielded her from her husband's death, that shielded her now from the thought of scandal and murder. *Faith,* she thought, and the word recalled her with a start. The sunburst clock above the mantelpiece said five minutes past eight. It told her that the program had been on for five minutes. It told her that her son had hurt her again, denied her five priceless minutes of solace.

Mrs. Sessions reached quickly through her pain for the radio, and turned it on. It came heavily and harshly alive. Space whistled and shrilled. She turned the dial past a murmur of music, a mumble of news, a scream of studio laughter. And then a quiet, reasonable voice said, "Because now is the time to be happy. Now. This day. This hour. This very moment. The past has vanished. It has gone, and we must let it go. It is no more. Let us turn our faces away from all that has gone before. There is no past. There is only the golden Now. Let us open our eyes to the peace and wonder of our bright dwelling. For . . ." Mrs. Sessions sighed. Here was the source of faith. This was the release that she had finally found after a lifetime of seeking and evasion. This was the fountain of wisdom that restored her and held back the alien, uncaring world. *Away from all that has gone before,* she thought, and closed her eyes. It was a personal message tonight. It was designed especially to her need. And to Leland's need. The thought led her mind abruptly beyond the reach of the soft and cultivated voice. She wandered back to uneasiness. She thought: *Why isn't he? Why can't he? Why?* The urgency of her want obliterated all of the milestones that had marked all of the years: the mechanical affection for the unwanted child, the long neglect and the periodic, conscience-stricken pamperings, the strict demands and the lavish gifts and the sudden punishments. Leland had been only one of her activities. He had taken his place with the Country Club, the Junior League, the Symphony Orchestra. She had watched his friends and had his teeth straightened and ordered his clothes from De Pinna's. She accused him from her unhappiness, and forced herself back to faith. She returned to the voice of reason: "Loving thoughts. Thoughts of love. For it is only in this way that we may manifest the good and the pure and the true."

Speaking of truth and reality and wisdom and strength of spirit, the voice purred peacefully on. Mrs. Sessions drifted on in its wake, toward serenity. The voice spoke of love and devotion, and she dreamily thought of Arthur. He had learned to play mah-jongg. He had taken an interest in the Symphony Orchestra. Arthur had always understood. He would have been willing to hold the right thought, and she had expected Leland to take his essential place. The voice slipped smoothly in, blocking the return of doubt. "Now is the time to remember our spiritual source. In giving thanks for our present good, we must not be impatient for the greater good. Impatience is a compound. It is the work of man. It is not an element in the Kingdom of God. For impatience only scatters good." Worry fell from Mrs. Sessions's mind like the memory of everything she wished to forget. She bravely took up certainty. *I'm his mother,* she thought, and knew that she only asked what every mother earned in the agony of motherhood. She knew again that faith and goodness and loving thoughts would triumph in the end. Peace grew like good in the room, and Mrs. Sessions sipped her tea. It was barely lukewarm now, but she didn't mind. She hardly noticed. She drank with faith and the voice of faith began to speak of error. Somewhere a violin whispered a benediction. The voice spoke the name of Jesus, and withdrew. Mrs. Sessions roused herself to turn off the radio. She couldn't risk distraction now. She wanted to be alone with her good unscattered, and Leland drawing close for the comfort of a mother's love. The clock above the mantelpiece ticked with the infinity of her patience. Far down the street, an automobile horn barked at the sultry night. Sophie climbed heavily up the back stairs. Mrs. Sessions drifted happily toward tomorrow. . . .

Mrs. Sessions awoke to confusion. Then memory returned. She had heard a car door slam. She thought: *I must have dropped off for a moment.* For verification, she peered at the clock. It was twenty minutes past ten. Before she could wonder, she heard the grate of a key in the front door lock. It pulled her stiffly to her feet. She hurried down the room to the hall.

"Leland?" she called. She was breathless with hope and anticipation. "Is that you, dear?"

Leland had his back to her. He was drawing his key from the lock. He closed the door and turned slowly around.

"Oh," he said vaguely. "Hello, Mother."

"Leland," she said. "Leland, dear. Oh, I'm so glad." She couldn't wait for him to come to her. Expectation demolished all her patience. She put out a hand. "I've been so worried. When you didn't come home to dinner, I began to imagine the most dreadful— You weren't very considerate, you know. To just wander off without a word. You might at least have called. I don't think that's asking too much."

Leland shook his head. "No," he said. "I know, Mother. And I usually do, don't I? But—"

"Leland!" She gave a kind of gasp. "Those clothes!" She hadn't noticed until now. She said with horror, "You didn't go out to dinner dressed like that? Without a coat or a necktie? In those filthy old sneakers! Really, Leland. I don't know what's come over you. To go out to dinner dressed like that."

"Look, Mother," he said. "If you'll just—"

"But Leland," she said. "How could you? Haven't you any pride? I know how terrible everything has been. I know what you've had to go through. But you know, dear, you simply mustn't let yourself—"

Leland said, "Mother! Would you like to know where I've been?"

The sharpness in his voice shook her like a contradiction. She had been prepared for contrition. But she forgave him. She was determined to comfort him, to demand a request for her sympathy.

"Why, of course, dear," she said. "Of course, I want to know." She let him see the wonderful understanding that she knew she had for him. "I realize you're not a boy any more. You have your own life. But it's just that I've been so worried. You left without a word, you know. Hours and hours ago. And I've been sitting here all alone. Don't you think you should be more considerate of your mother, dear?"

Leland said, "I'm trying to explain, Mother. If you want to know where I've been, I'll tell you."

Mrs. Sessions smiled a sad and sympathetic smile.

"Of course I do, dear," she said. "We'll go in the living-room where we can be comfortable, and you can tell me all about it. But you look so tired and warm, dear. Wouldn't you like to have a nice Coca-Cola? I believe I would. Why don't you just run out to the—?"

"Mother," Leland said. "Will you listen to me for just a second? The reason I didn't come home to dinner or call you or anything was because I couldn't. I've been down at the sheriff's office. I went for a walk around the block and a couple of deputies came along looking for glory. They picked me up. I guess they thought the police might have overlooked something. I've been answering questions since two o'clock this afternoon." He added, wearily, "I don't think they were terribly concerned about the way I was dressed. I doubt if they even noticed. They were too busy trying to beat the police to the prize."

Mrs. Sessions felt something give way. It might have been hope. But she held the smile on her lips, remembering patience, clinging to faith.

"You poor dear," she said. "It must have been dreadful." Yearning carried her on: "But really, Leland. That isn't a very nice way to talk to your mother. After all, dear, I was only thinking of you. I was only trying to help."

Leland looked at her. "Were you, Mother?" he said. He shrugged. "All right. I'm sorry."

"My poor boy," she said. "I know how awful it's been for you. I know so well. But we just won't think about it. We'll put all this ugliness out of our minds. We'll talk about something pleasant. Just the two of us."

Leland took a deep breath. "I don't think I feel much like talking, Mother." He moved away from the door. "If you don't mind, I think I'll just go on up to bed. I'm tired."

"I know, dear," she said. "Of course you are." She tried to swallow the lump of disappointment rising in her throat. She said with an effort, "I understand. I understand perfectly. But we don't have to talk. We'll just—" She put out a hand and clutched his arm. "I only want to help you."

Leland stood silent for a moment. Then he said, "Please, Mother. I—" He gently released his arm from her grip. "I don't want to talk. Or anything. I just want to go to bed."

"Leland," she said. It was almost a cry. She stared at him with a kind of desperate disbelief. It was as though her hope had bound him to an unbreakable promise. She said, "But I'm your mother."

Leland said, "I—" He shook his head. "Good night, Mother." He walked away, toward the stairs.

"You don't want me to help you," she said. The sound of the radio voice throbbed suddenly through her mind. It was the voice of treachery. She began to tremble. She cried out in a voice of accusation, "You don't care. Your own mother worries herself sick about you. She does everything in her power. But you don't care. You don't care about anything but yourself."

Leland halted at the foot of the stairs. He turned and faced her. He said sharply, "Stop it. For heaven's sake, Mother. I'm only going to bed. I'm tired and I want to go to bed. Good night."

"No," she said. "No." She didn't know what she meant. She hardly knew that she had spoken. She only knew that her son had denied her. She took a stumbling step. The harsh, ugly tears of age streaked down her face, and she was stripped of everything but hunger.

"But what about me?" she cried. "What about me?"

FIVE

THE CITY DESK SWITCHBOARD buzzed and buzzed. Without looking up from the brassière advertisements in an old copy of *Life,* the head office boy lifted an indolent hand to the thicket of plugs and broke the connection. A bead of sweat ran down his nose and dropped. It blurred a photograph of a chimpanzee in a high chair.

With a photographer at his side, Edwards faced Mr. Ramsey, the night city editor, across the desk. "He wouldn't be quoted," he said, and glanced at the photographer for confirmation. "But on the way out, we ran into Ferelli. He told me . . ." The city editor nodded, and drew a six-pointed star on his blotter. His vacation began the day after tomorrow.

At the copy desk, the copyreaders bent over their copy, marking the paragraphs in purple ink, deleting the adjectives, correcting the misspellings, clipping and pasting, alert for libel.

Coffman shouted into the telephone, "M like in mother?" He was wrangling with a down-state correspondent. "Y like in yesterday?"

Boyle jiggled the space bar on his typewriter and tugged at his right ear, seeking the one word that would precisely describe the moral indignation of the visiting archbishop.

LeFevre turned to the sports section of the Chicago *Tribune,* and relighted his cigar. He was waiting for something worthy of his attention. His coverage of the Finney kickback scandal in Kansas had brought him peace and plenty.

At the remotest desk, beneath the electric fan that was out of order again, Winger, impassive and unhurried, tapped out: *Mr. Ott leaves three daughters, Mrs. Alfred Karney Monmouth, 4219 Warwick Boulevard; Mrs. Francis J. Ford . . .*

After six years, Winger was still writing obituaries. He didn't really care. Winger had come a long way: from the journalism class of the Sedalia High School to the Kansas City *Times*. His salary was $100 a month and he lived on the top floor of a rooming-house four blocks from the nearest car line, but it was only a matter of time. Merit never passed unnoticed in the long run. Some night he would be the only reporter in the office. Edwards would be sick, Coffman would be off, Boyle would be busy on something that no one else could handle, and Brown would be out on an assignment. LeFevre would be in Topeka or Jefferson City or somewhere. Something would have happened to Prince and Stone and Beasely and McKay.

Winger wrote: *Funeral services will be held at 10 o'clock Wednesday at the . . .*

Mr. Ramsey would have no choice. Only Winger would be available. Behind the thick lenses the slightly protuberant eyes glazed with aspiration. His fingers died on the keys. Hope persisted in spite of everything: the managing editor who looked at him without recognition in the elevator, the indifference of the other reporters, the practical jokes of the office boys. Hope pushed all the evidence aside once more, and in his mind he saw Mr. Ramsey put down the telephone. The city editor's voice shook with excitement as he called to Winger. It was a sensational story. Winger stared blindly at his typewriter while his racing imagination plotted scandal and violence and mystery.

Winger saw himself firing crisp, corrosive questions at the police reporter who was telephoning from the scene. He saw himself striding back to his desk. The office boys stared. Winger had taken only a few cryptic notes. The details were stamped in his photographic memory. As he pulled up his chair, Mr. Ramsey came hurrying back and stood humbly at his side, waiting for the first smashing paragraph. The city editor lighted a cigarette with a trembling hand. He eyed the clock. "Good God, Winger," he breathed. "You've got less than three minutes to make the first run." But Winger, immune to excitement, merely smiled. "Don't worry, Chief—we'll make it all right." The lead went leaping across the page. Not a word was wasted. Not a pertinent fact omitted. It was brilliant, and original. Mr. Ramsey himself raced the first take up to the copy desk, exclaiming with delight as he ran.

The sound of his name penetrated the dream. Winger looked up, blinking through his glasses. He stumbled back to reality from the vision of the bloodstained Oriental dagger, the mysterious woman in black, the poisoned champagne cocktail, the bodies of the Governor and the Mayor sprawled at the foot of the fire escape of the disreputable North Side hotel.

The assistant city editor said, "Winger. There's a death on two."

Winger said nothing, and stood up. His face was expressionless. He had trained himself before the bureau mirror to unfathomability. With deliberation, making the most of his small height, he walked to the rank of telephones and lifted the receiver.

"Winger speaking," he said.

Someone in the office had once called him inscrutable. Winger had overheard, and denied the snickers. He stored the word away like a compliment in his private strongbox of facts and phrases and opinions. It popped into his mind now as he walked back to his desk with his eyes darting everywhere. *Inscrutable,* he thought, *the inscrutable Mr. Winger.* The sound of it in his mind was as impressive as ever. *The inscrutable Mr. Winger,* he thought again for good measure, and a flush of satisfaction glowed in the sallow cheeks of his oversize face. The mask of imperturbability was for the world that had not yet recognized him. It would also serve in the years of fame to come. Beneath the mask seethed a limitless, scattered ambition, a feverish determination toward accomplishment and acclaim: the best-selling novel, the syndicated column of sophisticated humor, the exclusive disclosures cabled from Berlin and Rome and Moscow. Winger had already completed almost two chapters of a story of Balkan intrigue and romance.

Boyle raised his head and emitted an authoritative yelp. An office boy strolled back for the fourth add on the visiting archbishop.

Hanging over the city desk, Coffman sorted out his notes, explaining everything to the city editor: "It sounds like a pretty good fire. Baker down at Moberly says it's already spread to . . ."

McKay called from the first desk to the boy at the switchboard, "Well, try his office at the Court House."

Winger's short bitten fingers moved methodically over the keys of his typewriter. *A firm believer in moderate exercise,* he wrote, *Mr. Ryan seldom missed his daily walk to his office.* He poked a wintergreen mint into his mouth and went on, embroidering the routine facts, dramatizing in vain the uneventful life.

A voice said, "There's no such address as this." It was a copyreader, the sullen, unshaven horseplayer who always handled Winger's copy. He waved a carefully typed paragraph. "Did you verify it?" He had just missed the daily double at Fairmount Park again.

Winger stared blankly through his glasses. His lips moved, but he said nothing. Thought formed uncertainly, inscrutably. Finally he was ready to reply. He said, "I thought—"

The copyreader dropped the folded sheet of paper onto the desk. He smiled with distaste at the only man on the city staff who was less essential than himself. "Suppose you check it again."

"Uh," Winger said. "I—" Nobody heard him. The copyreader had gone back to the copy desk. It didn't matter. The future stretched limitlessly ahead of him.

At the telephone rank, Prince was talking to somebody about a night-blooming cereus.

The city editor called, "Jerry. Judge Martin wants to add something to that statement. He's on seven."

LeFevre took his feet off his desk. "Okay," he said.

The mint dissolved on Winger's tongue. It was as sweet as a request for his autograph. Stolid and lifeless, his face bent over the typewriter, he wrote: *One of the charter members of the South Central Business Association, Mr. Ishmael served as* . . . But his mind was on a streetcar now. It was his night off. A furtive man with a twitching face slid into the seat beside him. Winger's mind vaulted over the opening remarks, the reason for trust, the introduction of the subject. It bounded to the heart of the matter: the slip of paper passed covertly into his hand, the muttered address, the incontrovertible evidence that the police, as usual, had been wrong, that it was Leland Sessions who had murdered Louise Heim.

Winger swallowed the last of the mint, and wrote: . . . *and a son, Morris T. Ishmael, of Mobile, Ala.* His mind jumped back to glory again. It soared in the twinkling of an eye through the tedious investigation, the questioning, the verification, the incredible stupidity of the police. It deposited him in the visitor's chair at the managing editor's desk, with Mr. Ramsey hovering at his elbow and the secretary warned that they were not to be disturbed by anyone. Then, in a few machine-tooled words, but without excitement, without even the habitual stammer, Winger revealed his astounding information, the true source of the Sessions fortune, the real identity of Louise Heim, the actual cause of death. "On the contrary, Boss," Winger remarked, and smiled. "I had a hunch all along that young Sessions was the chap to be watched. There was, if you recall, the detail of the crumpled match pack—"

"But," Mr. Ramsey said, "the police—"

"Nevermind, Fritz," the managing editor cut in. "Go

on, Mr. Winger. I'll admit it's astonishing, but everything you say fits perfectly. You've done a superb piece of work on this. Unless I'm very much mistaken, the Pulitzer Prize Committee . . ."

Winger accepted one of the managing editor's cigars and exhaled a long blue cloud of smoke. He began, with a dry chuckle and a courteous glance at Mr. Ramsey, to outline the way he planned to present the story. Behind him, at the far end of the room, the other reporters stood huddled together, watching the conference, wondering.

"Winger."

He started. Only the long discipline before the bureau mirror saved him from crying out. It was Mr. Ramsey calling him. But the city editor was seated at his own desk, and the managing editor had gone home hours ago.

"Winger."

The round, bulging eyes focused slowly through the dreams and the infinite, disordered ambitions.

"Here's some more information on the Erickson death," Mr. Ramsey said.

Winger sat motionless. He gave no sign that he had heard. He sat silent and inscrutable while the solution to the Heim case drained back into the dim churning recesses of his mind. It was hard to let it go. No other dream had ever been so vivid, so real, so provocative. It might almost have been a portent.

"On five," Mr. Ramsey said, and turned back in his chair.

SIX

LELAND SESSIONS lay curled in sleep in the mid-morning heat. His face was dark with stubble and sweat, and his mouth hung darkly open. Somewhere a screen door slammed. The dark head stirred, digging deeper into the damp and knotted pillow. A Manor Bakery wagon plodded along the curb. Above the grind of wheels and the stomp of hoofs rose the tiny piping of the driver's tiny whistle. Leland's hand moved feebly across the sheet. A child ran shrieking down the lawn next door, and another followed him, howling. Leland smiled. His groping fingers closed on nothing.

A dog, or one of the children, barked. Leland's lolling mouth fell shut. The smile vanished, as if he had swallowed it. He turned his head away from the light and groaned. He groaned again, and grunted, and slowly came awake. With his head still buried in the pillow, he listened to the familiar symphony of holiday-morning sounds. For an instant he was too comfortable even to stretch. And then reality struck. Memory bit into his bones. It wasn't a holiday. It was only an ordinary day—a Wednesday. But the distinction was academic. Every day was a holiday now. He rolled over onto his back and stared up at the ceiling and remembered who he was.

The children shouted and the tiny whistle shrilled, but

consciousness had carried him back again beyond their reach. They were lost in the thunder of memory. He gazed at the white, blazing emptiness of the ceiling. It was as far away as the vanished past. It might have been the future. He thought: *A year. A full year.* He stared up at twelve meaningless months of holidays. He had been able to endure the newspapers. He could almost forgive them, as he could almost forgive the police and the hidden looks and the sudden whispers of strangers. But he couldn't forgive that year. He could have faced the world from behind his desk. He could have smiled through his wicket into any gawking eye. He had taken a job, and found a career. It had become the one real satisfaction in his life. If they had only had the courage to let him keep it, it could now have been almost everything. It would have meant that he wasn't alone. It would have meant that someone believed in his innocence. Not even the police had gone further than threats and accusations. Even that cowboy detective had only knocked him down. They hadn't sat in judgment like his father's friend. They hadn't toyed with a pen and avoided his eyes and talked of friendship and fiestas and the Waldorf-Astoria. They hadn't condemned him on an assumption of guilt to a year of blacklisted idleness.

Leland kicked off the sheet. He sat up on the edge of the bed and plucked a cigarette from the crumpled package on his table. So much for friendship. But Carl Upjohn, with his cowardice and his cant, merely headed the list. There were others. He hadn't recorded every slight. There were some, like Billy Miles, of whom he had expected nothing. There were a few, like Abigail North, who had been busy the last three times he called, and Jack and Posy Huntting, who were away for the summer, as usual, at some Indian lake in Michigan, of whom he couldn't be sure. Well, he wouldn't call Abigail again. As for Jack and Posy, he could wait. They would declare themselves in the fall. But there were enough unequivocal cases. The list of former friends grew longer every week. *Friends,* he thought, and remembered the night before last in the tap-room of the Country Club. That made two more.

Tony Evans and Preston Smith were alone at the bar when he emerged from among the tables of the middle-aged diners. Leland joined them as he had so many times before. He remembered the casual salutes and the bar-tender's welcoming smile and the sweating drinks on the polished wood. Preston slid the bowl of potato chips into reach. Tony paused in the middle of a story, and retold it again from the beginning. For a moment, standing there with his glass in his hand, it was as though nothing had happened, as though this June had been like any other. Then, little by little, silence slowly settled. The three of them leaned against the bar with nothing more to say. They could have been strangers in a public place. They stared into the mirror, at the bartender wiping a glass, at the sporting prints on the wall. The air-conditioning unit choked on, like somebody clearing his throat. Preston looked elaborately at his watch.

"Well," he said. "I guess maybe we'd better push, Tony."

The bartender raised his head. He glanced at Preston, and reached for another glass.

"Yes," Tony said, and swallowed. "Yes—I guess so."

"You've got time for another drink," Leland said. Nothing could have been more natural. They were his friends. Except for Jack Huntting, Tony was the oldest friend he had. "One for the road."

"I'd like to," Preston said. "But the fact is, we're late now."

"Oh," Leland said, and suddenly the significance of the exchanged glances and the hesitation as the old friendship compromised with the new suspicion was all too plain. "Oh," he had said. It had been his last word. They had lingered, though, with what he knew was embarrassment. The old ties broke reluctantly.

"Well," Preston had said at last. "Take it easy, Lee."

"So long, Tony said. "See you later."

Maybe, Leland thought, and got up from the tousled

bed. *But not if I see you first.* He wondered what his two false friends had found to say to each other as they fled up the stairs and across the driveway to their car. He supposed it was only what everyone else was saying. It seemed incredible now that he had hoped for something different, that he could have thought there might be exceptions. His release by the police had been too inconclusive. He wondered when they would call him back again. He almost hoped that the next time would result in a formal indictment. It would give him a chance to defend himself. It would give him a chance to fight.

Leland combed his hair with his fingers and listened to the voices on the lawn next door. It was hard to believe they were only playing. He walked to the window and raised the shade and looked out. Two small boys were hilariously pawing each other around the trunk of a poplar tree. As he watched, they went suddenly silent. They squatted on their haunches and solemnly stared at each other. Then one of them gave a yelp. The other collapsed in a gale of grunts and cackles. Leland turned away. They, at least, weren't talking about him. But it wasn't sympathy. It was infancy. He opened the bedroom door and crossed the hall to his bathroom. The tile was cool under his bare feet. He closed the door and reached for the handle on the shower and gave it a savage wrench. He wished it were somebody's neck. . . .

Leland felt his way through the gloom of the pantry. The kitchen door was closed. He swung it back and stepped in. Sophie was sitting at the table, with a cup of coffee at her elbow and the morning paper folded open to the concluding installment of *Mr. Wife.* She looked up and uttered a cheerful snort.

"So," she said. "You're up."

Leland smiled at her. He picked up a chair and carried it over to the table and sat down.

"It's too hot to sleep," he said.

"I suppose you want some breakfast," Sophie said.

"Finish your coffee," Leland said. "I'm in no hurry. I

don't even know if I'm hungry." He nodded toward the paper. "Any news?"

"Fair and warmer," Sophie said. "No relief in sight."

"I suppose not," he said. "But that isn't what I meant. I meant news."

"I didn't notice," she said, and heaved herself to her feet. "I'll get you some orange juice."

Leland watched her shuffling away toward the refrigerator and felt a tug of affection. They were bound together by his childhood. His mother had corrected his table manners and chosen his clothes and sometimes called him into the living-room for a good-night kiss when she was entertaining. His father had set him chores and helped him with his homework and taught him how to drive a car. But Sophie had reared him. He reached for the paper and turned from *Mr. Wife* to the larger unrealities of the news section. There was nothing about the murder. There hadn't been for almost two weeks now. He supposed there wouldn't be until they called him in again.

The refrigerator door thumped shut. Sophie put a glass of orange juice in front of him and turned away to the stove. She came back with a cup of coffee and a plate of cinnamon rolls.

"You want something to go with that?" she said. "Some eggs?"

"I don't think so," Leland said. "It's too hot to eat." He took a swallow of orange juice. "Sit down and finish your coffee."

"I've got work to do," Sophie said, and sank into her chair. She added, "Your mother's gone out. I think it was another of those lectures. Like on the radio."

"Probably," Leland said.

"I wonder you could sleep," Sophie said. "She had me up and down stairs for a solid hour, helping to get her started. What I want to know is when *I'm* going to get some help. If she can run off to that temple every other day, it looks to me like she could find time to go down to the agency. These last three weeks have worn me out. I ache all over. I'll be sixty-two years old on the fourteenth day of August."

"I know," Leland said. "But maybe she already has. Maybe she can't get anybody." He began to butter a roll. "Maybe they're all afraid I'll slip downstairs some night and cut—"

Sophie said sharply, "Hush!" She shuddered. "If you're going to talk like that, you can leave my kitchen. I won't have it. Even in fun."

"I wasn't trying to be funny," Leland said. "I was only—"

"Then you're talking like a fool," Sophie said. "Which is worse. Everybody knows you didn't have anything to do with that nasty little snip. So stop it."

Leland looked at her, with gratitude. He hadn't realized the depth of her loyalty. But it was only loyalty. She hadn't faced a dozen detectives. She hadn't listened to Carl Upjohn. She hadn't heard Preston Smith and Tony Evans. She hadn't even seen that awful grinning scarecrow at the funeral. He said, "I don't know what you mean by everybody."

"There's always a few," Sophie said. "Some people will say anything. Just to hear their heads rattle." She picked up her cup and took an indignant gulp. "The rest have better sense."

"Good," Leland said. "But I wonder who they are. I haven't—" He glanced at her with a kind of bleak curiosity. "I wonder who they think it was."

"Think?" Sophie said. "I don't know why anybody would have to think."

In spite of himself, he stared.

"It's as plain as the nose on your face," she said. "What kind of a man would look twice at that kind of trash?" Her jaw hardened. "Nobody—except more trash."

"Oh," Leland said, and frowned. But it wasn't exactly disappointment. Something had brushed against his mind. "When you talked to the police," he said. He didn't quite know what he wanted to say. "Did you tell them that?"

Sophie nodded, but it was obvious that she hadn't heard.

She said with sudden venom, "When I think of what went on down there. All those months. Under my very nose. I used to let her lie down sometimes in the afternoon. She looked so tired. I only wish—" She shook her head.

"I know," Leland said. "But look, Sophie. Did you tell the police that? I mean, about the kind of man?"

"Of course I talked to the police," Sophie said. "And I picked up after them. If you could have seen that living-room." She took a deep breath. "No. I told them what I knew. I didn't tell them what I thought. They didn't ask me."

"No," Leland said. "I suppose not. But it wouldn't have made any difference anyway. They already had the man they wanted."

"Now stop that," Sophie said. "Do you hear me? Besides, that was then. That was three weeks ago. They know better now."

"Do they?" he said. He almost smiled. "They just haven't figured out a way to prove it yet. That's all. I'm not just talking. I'm telling you what I know. They're not even thinking of anybody else. And they won't. Not unless somebody drags him in and practically—" He stopped. He put a cigarette in his mouth and began to feel through his pockets for a match. "Or something like that," he said.

"There," Sophie said, in triumph. "That's exactly what I mean. And somebody will. Some detective. You wait and see." She smiled at him with satisfaction and finality. "That coffee must be stone-cold," she said. "I'd better get you some fresh."

"All right," he said. "I mean, no. I've had all I want." He shook his head, and tried to think. He said, "All those months—and you never heard a sound down there? You never saw anybody hanging around?"

"Oh, dear heaven," Sophie said with resignation. "I thought we— No, I never heard a sound. No, I never saw anybody. Do you think for a minute—"

"I know," Leland said. He looked at his cigarette. "Well —when she went out? She had dates. Didn't she ever say anything? Where she was going or who she was going to meet or anything like that?"

"I don't know," Sophie said. "Maybe she did. I don't remember. But I don't see why we— Besides, that was months ago. The last time she went out was I don't know when. Way back last winter. I used to feel sorry for her. I thought she was lonely."

"Well," he said. "She wasn't. At least we know that. But try to think. You saw her every day. You worked together. She must have said something. You must have talked to each other."

"Talk?" Sophie said. "Of course we talked. Or she did. I told you that. All she wanted to do was talk. But I couldn't be bothered. I had my work to do. It went in one ear and out the other. It was just talk—whatever popped into her head. Like the movies. And all about back home—that town she came from."

"Harrisonville," Leland said.

"Yes," she said. "Until I thought I'd go crazy. I guess she was homesick. She— No, I remember. It was some boy down there. They had a fight. But that was way back when she first came here. She stopped crying over him months ago. Before she stopped going out."

Leland sat up. "When was that?" he said. "You mean, about the same time she stopped going out? You mean, last winter? Around January or February?"

"It was around then," Sophie said. "I don't remember exactly. But it was after Christmas."

"Harrisonville," Leland said. "That's only about forty miles from here. You can drive it in an hour. Suppose they— Maybe he got in touch with her. Maybe they made up." He jabbed out his cigarette. He said, "Well, what did she say?"

"Say?" Sophie said. "About what? All I know is she just stopped going out. She didn't say anything."

"No," Leland said. "Of course not. Of course she wouldn't. I mean, if he was sneaking in here every night or so. Who would?"

"Dan," Sophie said. "That was his name. She called him Danny."

"Dan?" Leland said. "Dan what?"

"She never said," Sophie said. "Or if she did, I've forgotten. Danny is all I remember."

"Well, I guess it doesn't matter," Leland said. "I guess just Dan is enough. For now, anyway. Harrisonville isn't much of a town. Somebody down there would know." He broke off a piece of cinnamon roll, and dropped it back on the plate. He said, "What about those people she used to work for?"

"What about them?" Sophie said. "What are you talking about, anyway?"

"Who are they?" he said. "What was their name? I remember Mother mentioned it once."

"Hoyt," Sophie said. "They were named Hoyt. Something Hoyt. Why? What do you want to know that for? What makes you so interested in them?"

Leland shrugged. "I don't know," he said, and reached for his cigarettes. "I was just thinking. I thought maybe I might drive down there one of these days. I'd like to get a line on that Dan. I'd like to meet him. Maybe I could learn something."

SEVEN

THE HIT PARADE WAS ON THE RADIO in the apartment below. A trumpet called and the drums bent into a roll. An announcer shouted a name. The sound drove up through the floor, through the open windows, through the screens of the little balcony. It plunged like a boisterous, uninvited guest into the Drapers' crowded living-room.

But nobody noticed. Nothing survived the steaming heat, the solid, standing smoke, the shouted arguments, and the helpless alcoholic laughter. Somebody dropped a glass. The telephone rang and rang and rang. Somebody stepped on the Drapers' cocker spaniel. It slunk yelping under a chair.

Tommy Grear said, "Here's what I mean. Listen to this." He put another record on the portable phonograph that sat in everybody's way in the middle of the floor. "You and your Mildred Baileys," he said. The cast-iron voice of Bessie Smith began to sing:

> "He can be ugly, he can be black,
> So long as he can Eagle Rock and Ball the Jack,
> I want to be somebody's baby doll . . ."

No one listened. Even Tommy Grear wandered away. The voice of the dead woman went on and on. Presently the cornet took gently over. Then the voice complained once more, and gave up in despair. The needle began to scrape like a fingernail on a blackboard.

Somebody said bitterly, "You sound like the *Journal of Commerce*. What the Supreme Court actually said was . . ."

"The effect," Armstead said. "I'm talking about the effect."

On the sofa at the end of the room, Billy Miles sat solid and sweating between Dorothy Pickett and the girl from St. Joseph in the blue print dress. His moist blue eyes were withdrawing in fat and his scalp showed pink beneath the damp, thinning hair. He still had the remains of a powerful figure. The highball glass was like a thimble in his big red hand.

"Naturally I was interested," he said, and had to raise his slow, heavy voice to be heard. "Lee Sessions and I were down at Missouri together."

Dorothy Pickett said, "Oh, God, Billy. Are we going to have to hear all that again?"

"He was a Sigma Chi legacy," Miles said. "But he spent most of his time—"

Vernon Draper was leaning precariously over the coffee table, crushing out a cigarette. He straightened up and pushed his hair back off his forehead.

"Lee Sessions?" he said. "Where have I heard that name before?" He looked at Dorothy and laughed. Everything struck him funny tonight, even the drinks spilled on his carpet and the cigarette smoldering out on the window sill. "Did Billy mention Lee Sessions just now?" he said. "Or was that last Saturday night?"

"Okay," Miles said with tolerance. "Okay."

Dorothy said, "And I was hoping he'd tell us about the time he intercepted that Oklahoma pass."

"All right," Miles said, and took a sip of his drink.

The girl in the blue print dress said, "Did you really—?"

"Yes," Draper said. "Yes, indeed. Really and truly. On my Scout honor. Just ask him."

Miles smiled. These were his friends. He had been an usher at Dorothy and Denton Pickett's wedding four years ago. He and Vernon Draper worked for the same insurance company. He didn't mind what they said. He had seen the expected interest in the sooty black eyes, and the blue print thigh was warm and yielding against his hip.

He said placidly, "I remember one time Lee and I—"

"Lee," Draper said. "That tantalizingly familiar name."

The girl said, "Do you really think he—?"

Dorothy stood up, tall and thin and without grace. "And now," she said. "If you all will excuse me. This is approximately where I came in."

Somebody with a crew cut and horn-rimmed glasses came up and rested a hand on Draper's shoulder. He peered along the sofa. "Any you all see what happened to Eddie?" he said.

"Old Lee," Miles murmured. "He was a funny guy."

"But do you really think—?" the girl said. "I mean—"

"Well," Miles said, and let his elbow rest tentatively on the soft blue thigh. "It's hard to say."

"I find it hard to stay," Draper said, and exploded into laughter. He took a staggering retreating step. "I wish I could remember where I've heard that name before." He waved his long, quizzical face at them. "Was there something about him in the papers a few weeks ago?"

The girl opened her eyes and stared. "Why, good heavens," she said. "The papers were simply—" She stopped and giggled. "Oh," she said, and looked at Miles. "He's just— I thought for a minute he was serious."

Draper said, "Come on, Eddie."

The man with the crew cut nodded his head. "Okay," he said. "But if Eddie . . ."

Miles and the girl watched them go, disappearing into the laughter in the corner, into the argument in front of the fireplace, into the singing on the balcony, into the pounding brass of the Hit Parade.

"Did you really know Lee Sessions?" the girl said. "Or was that just kidding, too?"

Miles crossed his legs with dignity. He was always ready for surprise, but never for doubt. "Lee?" he said. "I thought I told you. We were down at Missouri together. We're old pals." He really believed it all now. In the three weeks since the murder of Louise Heim, the casual acquaintance had burgeoned into lifelong friendship. The indifferent greetings on the campus five or six years ago had become intimacy, the occasional cups of coffee together between classes, and the one drink together in somebody's parked car at a dance had all been transformed by celebrity into a hundred shared adventures. "Of course," he added, "I haven't seen a great deal of old Lee lately."

The girl nodded, watching him with a kind of fascination. He might have been Leland Sessions himself sitting there beside her. She wet her lips.

Miles shifted his bulk, and the provocative touch of the soft thigh went through him like a chill. He took a gulp of his drink. He smiled a warm, anticipatory smile. "You know how people drift apart," he said.

"I should say I do," she said. "There was a girl I used to know at Ward Belmont. We were together all the time. We were inseparable. And then—"

"Sure," Miles said quickly. He wasn't interested in her forgotten friends. "Of course," he said. "Lee and I see each other around. But you know what I mean. It isn't like it used to be down at school."

She said, "Have you seen him since—?"

Miles hesitated, and frowned, remembering the encounter in the parking lot ten days ago. He remembered the start of recognition in the familiar bony face and his own swiftly averted eyes, and the sense of shame that came later. "No," he said. "As a matter of fact, I haven't." He glanced briefly away. Something of that obscure shame still lingered. The sweet compulsion of the warm print thigh led him on to justification. "Naturally," he said, "I called him up as soon as I heard about it. I wanted him to know how I felt. You know."

"You did the right thing," the girl said. She was full of admiration. "It showed you were loyal."

Miles told himself that he had meant to. But it wouldn't have been fair, he thought. It would only have embarrassed him. Some things were better left unsaid. He relaxed. It wasn't as though he really believed that Leland Sessions had murdered Louise Heim. Memory shriveled, and another illusion joined the rest.

"It must have meant a lot to him to know," the girl said.

"Well," Miles said. The warm, sooty eyes swept away the last crumbs of discomfort. He let his arm rest lightly along the back of the sofa.

A sudden silence blew through the room like a breeze For an instant nobody moved or spoke. Then a voice said loudly, "Now wait a minute. Hold your horses. You can't compare Mussolini with Hitler." The phonograph started up again. Laughter revived in the kitchen.

"Old Lee," Miles said, and allowed his outstretched arm to sink slowly around her shoulders. She moved minutely in assistance. Across her back, the thin print stretched smooth and taut. There was no kind of a bulge. He thought: *She hasn't even got a brassière on.* Dryness tightened his throat.

Miles steadied himself with a ragged breath. He said, "I couldn't help feeling—" His voice hardly carried to his own ears. He cleared his throat. "I couldn't help feeling sorry for old Lee," he said. "I knew he'd take it hard. I remember down at school—" He had no idea what he was saying. He cleared his throat again. "Lee was a funny guy," he said. "When I picked up the paper that day—"

The girl said, "I read every word of it. And those pictures. Ugh." She stared at him avidly. "Do you really think he did it? I mean, you know him and all."

Miles reached across her lap to the coffee table and put out his cigarette. His hand wavered toward his drink, and then withdrew. It dropped gently on the round, warm thigh. He dragged the surface of his mind back to Leland Sessions.

"I suppose," he said with difficulty. "I suppose you read the medical examiner's report. He estimated she—"

"Yes," she said. "Yes. Of course I did."

"Well," Miles said. His hand crawled on around to the small soft swell of her breast. He had never felt anything so soft. She wasn't even wearing a slip.

"Go on," she said, and for a moment he didn't know what she meant.

"Well," he said. The usual words were ready. "I remember one time down at school. Lee was at a party and there was a girl from Arkansas there. I remember at intermission—" He would have preferred some other way. But there wasn't time tonight. He couldn't wait.

"What happened?" the girl said.

Miles compressed his lips, and shrugged.

"Oh, hell," he said, with inflaming reticence. "It isn't really fair." He gestured vaguely. His hand fell back, a trifle higher on her thigh. He waited to be sure. But she gave no sign that she was aware of the pioneering fingers.

She said, "Tell me."

"I shouldn't have mentioned it," Miles said. "Let's forget it. Let's talk about something else."

"No," she said. "No. Please tell me."

"It wouldn't be fair," he said. "You know it wouldn't be fair."

"No," she said. "Yes— I mean, I won't breathe a word of it. Honestly, I won't." She was breathless. "Tell me."

Miles reached boldly into the giving breast. It was like an involuntary gesture. Certainty gave his voice its normal depth and strength. "But Lee's a friend of mine," he said. "It wouldn't be right to bring a thing like that up now."

"I won't tell a soul," she said. Her eyes were as bright and hard as metal. "I promise I won't."

"I know," Miles said. He tightened his encircling arm, and felt her tremble and respond. "But it probably didn't mean anything. Besides, that was almost six years ago."

"Then you can tell me," the girl said. "I understand how you feel, and I admire you for it. I really do. But tell me. Please."

Somebody came through the doorway from the kitchen,

and fell down. The whisky from the shattered glass soaked darkly into the carpet. Somebody laughed and somebody stared. But nobody was really interested. It had happened too many times before.

"Besides," Miles said. "There was never any proof. There was only—" He could not recall whether he had said Arkansas or Oklahoma. "There was only that girl's word for it."

"What did she say?" the girl said. "What happened?"

Miles felt the hidden nipple stiffening beneath the thin print. The girl moistened her thin, eager lips. Miles abruptly took his hand away.

He said, "I'm about to suffocate. All this smoke— You could cut it with a knife."

The girl looked at him.

She said, "It is—warm."

Miles stood briskly up. Leland Sessions was abandoned on the sofa until the next time. "My car's out front," Miles said. "What we need is a little air."

He hadn't the least doubt now.

The girl said, "Well—"

Their hands closed hotly together. Miles grinned, and helped her up.

EIGHT

Leland mounted the steps and crossed the broad, shadowy veranda. The dry boards creaked at every step, like a warning to reconsider and retreat. Under the sweltering weight of the old felt hat, sweat prickled up through the prickly stubble of the unfamiliar crew cut. The glasses that he sometimes wore for reading hung hot and heavy on his nose, dimly distorting everything. He wondered if his attempts at disguise looked as transparent, and as uncomfortable, as they felt. But he couldn't turn back now. He was committed by more than the stop for directions at the filling station on the square or the sight and sound of his arrival. He was also bound by two days of planning, and hope.

The screen door was closed and latched, but the inner door stood open, stopped by a carpet-covered brick. Just inside was a small table surmounted by a large bowl full of visiting cards. Beyond the table was the beginning of a flight of stairs and the twilit depths of a hall. Leland hesitated. There was no bell. He raised his hand and rapped on the panel of the screen. There was a sudden crash of cutlery. A drawer slammed, and then a door. The darkness stirred at the end of the hall. Leland straightened his shoulders and squared his jaw. A Negro girl in white socks and red moccasins came slowly into view. She peered through the screen.

"Oh," she said. It was as if she had expected someone else. "Yes?"

Leland cleared his throat.

"Is Mrs. Hoyt at home?" he said.

"I don't know," she said. "What was it you wanted to see her about?"

"I'm a reporter," Leland said. He touched the row of pencils in his breast pocket. They might have been his credentials. "My name is—Chase."

"Oh," the girl said. She gave him a look that could have meant anything. "You mean from the newspapers?"

"The *Journal*," he said. "I'm from Kansas City."

"Well," she said, and turned away. "I'll go see."

Leland tried to think how he had planned to begin. He tried to remember how the reporters had talked to him. But he couldn't. There had been no way of knowing that morning in the living-room exactly who the reporters were. Everyone had looked like a detective. Somewhere out of sight a clock struck a quarter hour. He looked at his watch. It said five minutes to two. The deeps of darkness stirred again.

"Mrs. Hoyt says to come on back," the girl said. She unlatched the screen door. "She's out in the garden."

The girl led the way, past the table, past the stairs, and down a long, musty passage. Leland followed her blindly, with his heart in his mouth. They turned an unseen corner.

The girl pulled open a door and flattened herself against a sudden tier of shelves. He squeezed around her and stepped out onto a teetery flagstone walk and into a blaze of sunlight.

A tall, muscular woman with a peeling nose and a tangle of iron-gray hair rose up from a clump of zinnias. She had on pink denim shorts and a black silk halter. She came cheerfully toward him, swinging a trowel.

"Mr. Case?" she said. "Is that right—Case? I never know. Poor Susan mumbles so."

"Chase," Leland said. He tried to look as though it

really mattered. "John Chase. I'm—"

"Chase," she said, as if she intended to remember it. "Well, needless to say, I'm Buffie Hoyt." She extended a grimy hand. "I hope you'll excuse the way I'm dressed. This is my gardening costume. Or so-called. Gardening is my passion. Unrequited, though, I'm afraid. I'm always two jumps behind the weeds. My husband says I have a brown thumb." She laughed heartily.

Leland smiled.

"However," Mrs. Hoyt went on briskly. She tossed the trowel under a bench. "I'm sure you didn't come all the way from Kansas City to talk about that."

"Well, no," Leland said. He renewed his smile. "I—"

"Unless I'm very much mistaken," Mrs. Hoyt said, "it's about that awful murder. Personally, I think the less said about such things the better. But I know how you newspaper reporters are. I should—you're the third one that's been to see me since it happened. Although I must say the others got here a little faster than you did. Or are you one of the same ones back again? I thought for a minute when you came out of the house that you looked a little familiar. But I suppose that's just my imagination. Or, more likely, my age. All you young men are beginning to look alike to me."

"I guess that's it," Leland said hastily. "We—" Alarm subsided into embarrassment. "I mean, we probably do look all alike." He hurried on to safety. "But what I wanted to talk to you about isn't so much the murder. It was about Louise Heim herself. I'm supposed to write a sort of story of her life. You know, where she was born and where she went to school." He plucked a pencil for his pocket and reached for the notebook that he had bought that morning. "Who her friends were—that sort of thing." He smiled encouragingly. "A kind of biographical article."

"I see," Mrs. Hoyt said. "Or rather, I don't. Wasn't all that in the papers? I'm sure the *Star*—"

"Well, yes," Leland said. He poked the pencil back into his pocket, and carefully chose another. "Some of it was.

But there must be a lot of little details about what she was really like. I mean, to people like you that really knew her. I thought it would be very interesting to have your impression of her."

"Oh," Mrs. Hoyt said. "Oh, I see. I'm sorry—you'll have to forgive me for being so obtuse. Impressions are all the rage now, aren't they? We used to call them character sketches." She leaned against a tree. "Poor Louise. Well, my impression was favorable. Entirely so. I was really very fond of her. Of course, she wasn't terribly bright. She— But maybe you'd better not write that in your article. Let's just say that I found her very willing and a good, hard worker. To tell the truth, I was quite surprised. I prefer colored help. They need more keeping after, but, as a rule, they're better workers. So when Mr. Ludermann spoke to me about Louise, my impulse was to say no."

"Mr. Ludermann?" Leland said.

"Joseph Ludermann," Mrs. Hoyt said. "I think you ought to write that down. It's L-u-d-e-r-m-a-n-n. He might be a good one for you to see. A lot of us thought he was Jewish when he first came here, but he isn't. Two n's makes it German, you know. He's the principal at the high school and a very fine man."

Leland nodded. "That's very interesting," he said.

"Yes," Mrs. Hoyt said. "Of course, I'd known Louise for years. I mean, I knew of her. Buck Heim was on the fire department almost ever since I can remember. It was really terribly tragic. As you probably know, he and Louise's mother died within mere weeks of each other. That was back in 1931. So, naturally, Mr. Ludermann was vitally interested in poor Louise. She had no one else to turn to. He's that kind of man. Which was probably why I finally agreed. But, as I say, I never regretted it. Louise had her faults. She was a little what I call moony. I'd find her standing in the middle of the living-room with a dustcloth in her hand, just dreaming. On the whole, though, she was very satisfactory. And an extremely nice girl. Or was when I knew her, that is. Of course, I can't speak for—"

"No," Leland said. "Of course not. I understand that." He hesitated. "Although I did hear that she had some kind of an affair. Wasn't there some man just before she came up to Kansas City? I think I've got a note here—" He glanced at his notebook, and turned a page. "As I recall, his first name was Dan."

"Dan?" Mrs. Hoyt said. "Oh—you mean Danny. Danny Dodge. But I—"

"That's it," Leland said. "Danny Dodge. I suppose you know him?"

"Everybody knows Danny," Mrs. Hoyt said. "He used to be a fixture down at Mitchell's—the big hardware store on the square. He and Bub Peters have a little radio repair shop now. But I'd hardly say that he and Louise had an affair. Not what I'd call an affair, at least. They simply went together for a year or so. As far as I know, they were just good friends."

"I'm sure that's all it was," Leland said. "Besides, I'm not interested in that sort of thing, anyway." He looked thoughtful. "But I was just wondering. Do you know where his shop is? I thought maybe if I have time, I might look him up before I leave. I don't suppose he could add much to what you've told me, Mrs. Hoyt. You've been very helpful. But it might be worth trying."

"Well, I don't know about that," Mrs. Hoyt said. "I mean, whether I've been very helpful or not." She pulled gently at her nose. "But I do believe I've given you a very fair impression of Louise. She was one of the most willing girls I've ever had. And I think that's terribly important. So many girls just won't try. I think I understood her, too. Most of her trouble was simply shyness. Once I realized that, we got along beautifully. Right up to the very end. And when the day came when she decided to leave—well, to be quite frank, I was sorry to see her go. Even if she was up in the clouds half the time." Mrs. Hoyt grinned. "But, of course, they're all like that."

"Yes," Leland said, and managed an arid chuckle. "I suppose so. And that's very interesting about her shyness.

Everything else, too. You've really given me exactly what I want." He gazed blindly at his notebook and prayed for patience. He said, "Oh, yes—about Danny Dodge." It was impossible that she couldn't sense the urgency in his voice. "I believe you said he had a radio shop. Is that—?"

"It's a radio repair shop," Mrs. Hoyt said. "Or so I've heard. I've never actually been in it. But it's quite a good one, I understand. Bub Peters is very clever."

"Oh," Leland said. He tried again. "I wonder if I passed it on the way here. Is it down on the square, too?"

"I don't imagine you did," Mrs. Hoyt said. "Not unless you came the long way around. It's about a block south of the square—just beyond that big Cities Service station. You can't miss it. But if I were you, Mr. Case, I wouldn't waste much time on Danny Dodge. I suggest you go see Mr. Ludermann. I'm sure he would be far more helpful."

"Oh, I intend to," Leland said. "And I'm very grateful to you for telling me about him." He closed his notebook. "I just thought I'd see Danny Dodge—you know, if I had time." He held out his hand. "I don't know how I can thank you, Mrs. Hoyt."

"Then don't try," Mrs. Hoyt said. She laughed. "At least, that's what my father always used to say. But, seriously, I've enjoyed it. Anything to keep me off my hands and knees."

"Well," Leland said. The smile ached on his face. "Thanks again."

He began to back away.

Mrs. Hoyt stooped to retrieve her trowel. "Oh," she said, and stared suddenly up. "By the way—"

Leland froze.

"The paper you write for," she said. "I believe Susan said the *Journal*. Well, we don't often see the *Journal*. But, of course, I wouldn't want to miss your write-up. I mean, naturally, I'm terribly interested. Will it be in to-morrow, do you think?"

"Why," Leland said, "I—" Relief left him too weak to think. "I—it's hard to say. But sometime this week, I suppose. Or maybe next." He promised wildly, "I'll let you know."

"Would you?" Mrs. Hoyt said. "That would be so nice. And I'm sure it will be a simply wonderful article."

"I'll send you a card," Leland said, and backed heavily into a tree. He sidled around it. A path wandered through a jungle of lilac and on toward the front of the house. It was all he could do not to run.

Elation rode beside him all the way back to the square. He tried to remind himself that his interview with Mrs. Hoyt had actually clarified nothing. She had hardly been more than just another guide. Like Sophie and the filling-station attendant on the corner, she had only supplied him with a name and told him where to go. But he couldn't listen to reason. It had been a test of courage and inge-nuity, and he had faced it. He had emerged safe and vic-torious. He grinned up at the big, ugly, yellow bulk of the Cass County Courthouse, and felt like shouting. Mrs. Hoyt had armed him with confidence in John Chase of the *Journal*. He was ready for Danny Dodge.

Leland turned off the square. A great, glittering oasis of concrete, bristling with pumps and strung with pennants, beckoned from the end of the block. He drove slowly past and into a dingy street of parked cars and false-front stores and gaunt gray rooming-houses. The shop was halfway down the block: *P. D. Q. Radio Repairs & Service*. A loud-speaker was perched like a birdcage over the entrance and a dismembered packing crate lay at the curb in a pool of spilled excelsior. Leland pulled up in front of a second-hand furniture store a couple of doors beyond. A woman with a pencil in her hair peered at him through the glass from behind a barricade of purple overstuffed chairs. He stared reluctantly back, and felt his resolution falter. He wrenched it back with a cigarette and swung open the door and got out. Mrs. Hoyt had accepted him without ques-tion. It was inconceivable that Danny Dodge would be any more difficult to deceive. If anything, he told himself, this was the simpler task. He wasn't seeking information. He didn't expect to surprise an admission of guilt. He only hoped to surprise a look or sense a ripple of fear. The police would do the rest.

A gust of studio laughter blew down the street to meet him. Leland quickened his steps. The laughter petered out in a crash of steel guitars. He ducked under a cascade of *La Cucaracha*. The door of the shop was ajar. He pushed it open and walked into a small, gritty room crammed with cluttered shelves and ravaged radios. A young man in a grimy T-shirt sat crouched on a stool at a workbench in a corner. He raised his head and slid to his feet. He was pale and stooped and scrawny, and there was a skull-and-crossbones tattooed in blue on one of his bony, blue-veined arms.

"Yes, sir," he said in a faraway voice. He touched a button on the underside of the bench. The music sank to a tinkle. "What can I do for you?"

"I wanted to see Mr. Dodge," Leland said.

"That's me," the man said, and sighed. "At your service."

"Oh," Leland said. He tried to mask his astonishment with a smile. So this was Louise's lover. He stared at the sagging shoulders and the sunken cheeks and the hollow, lifeless eyes. But he might not have looked like this then. He wondered if he could be looking at the dilapidations of guilt. His heart gave a heave. He said carefully, "My name is Chase—John Chase. I'm a reporter for the *Journal*."

"Yeah?" Dodge said.

"I wanted to talk to you about Louise Heim," Leland said. "I'm writing a kind of story of her life. I understand you used to know her."

"Yeah?" Dodge said. "Who told you that?"

"Told me?" Leland said. "Is it supposed to be a secret?" He smiled a disarming smile. "But, as a matter of fact, it was Mrs. Morton Hoyt. I've just come from talking to her."

"She did, eh?" Dodge said. "Mrs. Hoyt." A kind of satisfaction glittered in his eye. "She sent you to me? Well—"

He shrugged. "Okay. I knew Louise. What about her?"

Leland took out his notebook. "Nothing in particular," he said. "As I say, I'm writing this article about her. What she was really like—you know. Mrs. Hoyt gave me her impressions of her. I thought it would be interesting to hear how she impressed you."

"Yeah?" Dodge said. "What did she say—Mrs. Hoyt, I mean?"

"Why, she liked her," Leland said. "She said she was a nice girl—a hard worker."

Dodge nodded. "Yeah," he said. "Louise was okay. She was a good kid. We had some good times together." He glanced at Leland. "How's that?" he said. "Is that what you want?"

"That's fine," Leland said. He made an elaborate note. "Uh—you knew her for quite a while, I gather?"

"About three years," Dodge said. "But, look. If you want to talk to me some more, I've got to sit down. I just got out of the hospital. I'm still as weak as a cat."

"Sure," Leland said. "Go right ahead. I thought— I mean, you look as if you'd had some trouble."

"Trouble!" Dodge said. He dropped limply down on the stool. "I damn near died." He said with pride, "I had trichinosis. You know what that is?"

"No," Leland said, and wet his lips. "No, I guess I don't."

"You get it from eating pork," Dodge said. "Or can, if it isn't cooked enough. It's like a worm. They get in your muscles. You get enough of them in there, and you really know it. I was out like a light for two whole days."

"Oh," Leland said. His stomach suddenly tightened. "When was that?"

"You mean, when was I knocked out?" Dodge said. The question seemed to invigorate him. "Let's see." He scratched his head with an oily thumb. "That must have been right around the first of June. Yeah—they took me to the hospital on Decoration Day. I remember that, and I remember waking up the next morning and wondering where the hell I was. But that's about all I do remember until I came out of it. I guess I went under that afternoon." He said in admiration, "They said I didn't hardly move a muscle for over forty-eight hours."

Leland opened his mouth. But he couldn't trust himself to speak. He swallowed.

"But I'd been dragging around for a couple of days before that," Dodge said. "Before they took me to the hospital, that is. That's where they decided it was trichinosis. They never did figure out where I got it, though. One of doctors said probably a hamburger. Which is possible. I used to practically live on them. But not any more. I've had my lesson. Most of the damn things are half pork. Did you know that?"

Leland shook his head. He said, faintly, "Decoration Day was a month ago."

"You're telling me?" Dodge said. "I was flat on my back for twenty-three days. They only let me out last Friday. Bub—that's my partner—he was practically off his rocker. This isn't the biggest business in town, but I don't mind saying it's more than just one man can handle. To tell the truth, I shouldn't even be here today. I'm as weak as a cat still."

"Yes," Leland said. He made one last effort. "Which— what hospital were you in?" But he knew it was no use. He couldn't doubt that there was a hospital. It was impossible to question the evidence that looked haggardly up at him from the stool. He knew he had seen and heard the truth.

"I was up at St. Luke's," Dodge said. "Old Doc Lemon—" A telephone at his elbow emitted a sudden, ear-splitting peal. He gave a start and a grunt. "That's probably Bub now," he said, and swung listlessly around on his stool.

"Look," Leland said. The telephone exploded again. It revived him like a reprieve. He said, "I'd better come back some other day. I mean, when you're not so busy."

"What?" Dodge said. "Just a second—" He put out an

arm and heaved the receiver off its cradle. "Hello?" He gazed at Leland doubtfully.

"Besides," Leland said. He began to move toward the door. "You've given me just about everything I need."

"Yeah?" Dodge said into the telephone. "Well— Say, hold it, will you?" He said to Leland, "But I thought—"

"No," Leland said. "Never mind. You go on with your work." He raised a smile. "I'll see you later."

"Yeah?" Dodge said. "Well—" He shrugged. "Okay."

Leland found the door and wrenched it open, and stumbled blindly out. The sun struck him like a blow. He tried to tell himself that it didn't matter. He tried to believe that he was only back where he had started. But there was no use even pretending. He hadn't called on Mr. Ludermann. He wouldn't send Mrs. Hoyt a card. There would be no article in the *Journal*. He had scarcely the strength to open the door of his car. He slumped into the seat and fumbled for the starter. He had found a way to fight back and he had taken it. He told himself that he had done his best. He wondered if he could possibly have done worse.

PART TWO

ONE

Winger crept cautiously down the dim, familiar stairs. He paused in the twilit entrance hall and stared at nothing, and listened. Somewhere overhead a toilet flushed. The old house quaked and groaned in the distant, strangling clamor. Someone walked heavily down the uncarpeted third-floor hall. A door opened and closed. That would be Mr. McGreevy. Winger cocked his ear for a more immediate threat. But nothing stirred behind the drawn portieres and the closed sliding doors of the parlor where Mrs. Lebrecht lived with her cats and her bedridden husband. He was alone.

Winger blinked slowly around the silent hall. The time had come. Like Mr. McGreevy and Mrs. Lebrecht, everyone was accounted for. He had waited at his window all through the afternoon, watching the comings and goings, identifying the steps on the stairs, and he knew. They were all of them out, or withdrawn to their rooms, for the evening. He savored the moment with a fleeting, secret smile. Then he slipped stealthily around the newel post and into the alcove beneath the stairs. He picked up the telephone. In the economical glow of the night light, the scarred wall crawled with a hundred scribbled numbers. Winger smiled with contempt at the litter of lazy minds. He could rely on his memory. It had been trained by mail at a school in Seattle. The number he wanted stood as unshakable in his mind as ambition. He thrust a shaking finger into the dial and eased it slowly and silently up and around. Secrecy, at this stage, was everything. No one must know that Winger was on the track of an exclusive story. No one must know that he was pitting himself against a cunning and a ruthless murderer. Far away, across the city, he could hear the other telephone ring.

There was a sound of footsteps on the porch. Someone was coming. Winger quickly replaced the receiver. Driving all expression from his face, he stepped quietly into view. The loose pane rattled as the front door came open. It was Mr. Jerome. Winger had miscalculated, but he didn't reproach himself. He almost welcomed the interruption. It merely prolonged the suspense. He waited with a kind of exhilaration for Mr. Jerome to see him. For an instant Winger saw himself as he knew the other would—a man of mystery, standing quietly in the stair well, cool, courteous, and impenetrable. He searched the immobile face and the inscrutable eyes behind the thick lenses, and was baffled.

"Oh," Mr. Jerome said. He gave a delicate start. "I didn't notice you for a moment, Mr. Winger."

Winger said carefully, defeating the stammer, "Good evening, Mr. Jerome."

Mr. Jerome patted his forehead with a damp handkerchief. "My," he said, "it's warm tonight. And they say there's no relief in sight."

Winger felt for a cryptic answer, a climactic thrust. His mind churned among the alternatives, but excitement trapped his tongue. He stood vigilantly silent.

"Perhaps," Mr. Jerome said, gripping the banister, "we'll have a little breeze later on."

He trudged on up the stairs, carrying his faded straw hat and his mild hope. Winger watched him disappear around the corner of the landing. He permitted himself a self-congratulatory smile. His instinct was infallible. He had said precisely enough. Another word would have dulled the total effect. He had spoken with impeccable courtesy, but with a puzzling suggestion of something withheld, the slightly unsettling reticence of a newspaperman whose lips are sealed.

Winger loitered for a moment in reverie. Then duty abruptly recalled him. He took a step toward the telephone. But the interruption had left him restless. It wasn't safe to count on privacy here. He hadn't supposed that Mr. Jerome would return so soon from his walk. He wondered if it might not be wiser to use the telephone at the drugstore. His mind heaved and settled and relaxed. The mysterious untraceable call from a public telephone would be a polished professional touch. Winger thought of the clerks and the customers watching him as he stood secretly in the booth. The thought made him blink with pleasure.

Anticipation insulated him from the heat all the way down the long block to the drugstore on the corner. At the door, he paused for reflection. An entrance was always important. Should he move fast and fierce and full of urgent purpose? Or would a quiet deliberation be more effective? He studied a display of dentifrices, and decided in favor of the latter. There was no need yet for haste. He held the door for a woman with a limp, smoothed the lapels of his double-breasted blue serge suit and touched the brim of his Homburg hat, and followed her sedately in. He glanced once at a mirror to assure himself that his face revealed nothing, not even his age, and then looked at no one.

Winger left curiosity to the others. He closed the door of the booth and settled on the tiny seat. The tiny fan began to hum, stirring the stifling air. He slowly dialed the number.

The faraway telephone rang again. Winger stared at the wall and waited. The faraway receiver clicked.

A woman's voice said, "Mrs. Sessions' residence."

"Uh," Winger said. He found it necessary to clear his throat. "I'd like to speak with Mr. Leland Sessions."

"Mr. Sessions?" the woman said. "Just a moment. I'll call him."

There was a pause. The line hummed with emptiness. A man's voice said, "Hello?"

Winger took a deep breath. "Mr. Sessions?" he said. He was alert to the possibility of a trick. "Is this Mr. Leland Sessions?"

"Yes," the man said. "This is he."

"Uh," Winger said, and found himself faced with a decision. Should he identify himself? Or should he merely give his name. He compromised. "This is—Winger."

"What?"

"Winger," Winger said. "My—my name is Winger."

"Yes?"

"Uh," Winger said, and racked his brain. He couldn't think what to say next. "I don't believe you know me."

"No," Sessions said. "No—I don't believe I do."

"No," Winger said. A bead of sweat seeped out from under his hat and trickled down his cheek. He said with inspiration, "But you will."

"Would you mind speaking a little louder?" Sessions said. "I didn't hear what you said."

"I said," Winger said thickly, "you would. You will."

"Oh," Sessions said. "But I'm afraid I don't know what you're talking about."

"Murder," Winger said. He heard himself with astonishment, and delight. He said, "I'm talking about murder."

"I see," Sessions said. "Well, suppose you go to hell."

The line went dead. Sessions had hung up. Winger slowly replaced the receiver and pushed open the door. The sweat was streaming down his face, but he hardly noticed. He was too startled by his daring to be aware of discomfort. His recklessness filled him with awe and admiration. Winger had laid his cards on the table. He had given fair warning.

At the soda fountain, he treated himself to a limeade. He needed it. He was weak. Only the rigorous training kept the bursting exhilaration from showing itself in his face. With his short legs swinging from the high counter stool and the cool straw between his lips, Winger relived the moment of his inspiration. The curse it had wrenched from the murderer's lips was proof enough that the blow had struck and been felt. He tipped up the glass and crunched a particle of ice, and slid down from the stool. It was just as well that Sessions had given him no time to request a meeting and an interview. A talk, at this point, would be premature. There was time for that later. *The war of nerves,* he thought. *First, the war of nerves.*

He began to readjust his plans as he walked reflectively up the noisy, darkening street to the rooming-house. There were not many changes necessary in the master pattern. The revised plan would be little more than an intensification of what he had done before. For more than a month, Winger had devoted much of his leisure to Leland Sessions. He had roamed the downtown streets during a dozen noon hours in the hope of encountering him, and observing his movements. He had seen him once. It was only a glimpse, and he had lost him a moment later, but it had been enough to confirm all of his suspicions. Winger could recognize guilt as readily as the shape of a criminal head.

But those hours of purposeful wandering had also shown him his own limitations. He could no longer afford to leave their encounters to chance. Winger gazed down at his feet and told himself that he had to have a car. He had to know where Sessions went and whom he met and what he did, and for that a car was essential. He couldn't stalk him on foot. The thought of the cost made his head swim, but he faced it squarely. Any kind of a car would do. The used-car lots that he passed on the way to work were full of bargains. He considered his savings, and the possibility of moving back to the Y.M.C.A. If that wasn't enough, he might even sell his typewriter. No sacrifice was too great. He would be amply repaid in the end. LeFevre had received a bonus of five hundred dollars for merely his coverage of the Pendergast trials. Winger's thoughts took flight. They soared away through bonuses and raises and by-lines and his picture on the cover of *Time.*

Winger was back in his room beneath the eaves before he was able to concentrate again on the revision of his plans. He stripped down to his BVDs and ran quickly through his exercises. His mind strained with his muscles. His vacation began a week from Sunday. Some explanation could be found to satisfy his parents in Sedalia. Two full weeks would give him all the time he needed. Tonight he had given fair warning. A week from Sunday the eternal watching would begin. He had only to follow and listen and observe, and then, at the psychological moment, would come the sudden confrontation, the cool, knowing interview, and the end. Winger peered at himself in the wardrobe mirror. His reflection peered stolidly back, inscrutable even in triumph.

TWO

Mr. Foley opened the rear door and looked out into the beer garden. There was nobody there. The dusty metal chairs and tables sat abandoned in the graveled court. Along the enclosing walls the honeysuckle drooped, frail with drought. The August moon hung big and bright over the roof of the laundry beyond the vacant lot next door, and everywhere the cicadas rang like bells.

Mr. Foley stared at the emptiness, and wondered why he had come out. He hadn't expected to find anyone sitting here on a night as hot as this. The thermometer on the nail by the door said ninety-five. He looked at it again to make sure. But ninety-five was right. He felt a stir of curiosity. Letting the screen door slam behind him, he moved heavily across the crunching gravel to the nearest table. The top of the table was still warm. It was almost hot.

"Ye gods," Mr. Foley said. He wiped his hand on his trousers and sighed. He wouldn't have believed it possible. Mr. Foley had lived in Kansas City for twenty-three years, but the summers still took him by surprise. Winter was Mr. Foley's season. He was insulated against the cold. *Ninety-five,* he thought, with a kind of horrified delight. He shook his wide, pink face. He walked slowly back to the door.

The familiar damp, smoky coolness closed comfortably

around him. *Foley's* was air-conditioned. The cost was staggering, but the salesman had been persistent. Mr. Foley couldn't say no to anybody. The cool air that washed expensively through his place, the pile of worthless checks in the cash drawer, the monumental juke box, and the elaborate neon sign out front all were testimonials to his acquiescence. But his weakness was his luck. The stuffy bar down the street was dragging along to bankruptcy. His tolerance sometimes shamed somebody into making good on one of the checks. The big sign beckoned and the phonograph was too magnificent to be ignored.

With the sweat chilling pleasantly under his striped shirt, Mr. Foley went along the passage, past the storeroom and *Men,* past *Ladies* and the kitchen, and on toward the bar. The journey into the garden had drained him like a violent exercise. He sighed in the passage. He might have been on the verge of collapse. But it was a sigh of satisfaction. Life came back with the dark smell of beer and the mutter of voices.

Behind him, the door of *Men* creaked open.

A voice said, "All I said was about her legs. I only said they were good."

"I know," another voice said. "He's funny that way. But he's really a wonderful fellow."

Mr. Foley turned and smiled at them. The one in the tan seersucker suit was a stranger to him. But Mr. Foley smiled at them both impartially.

"I just happened to look at the thermometer," he said. "It's ninety-five right now. Ninety-five degrees."

"Is that right," the stranger remarked.

The other man only nodded.

"Yes, sir," Mr. Foley said. "Ninety-five degrees." He stepped aside to let them pass.

"When you get to know him," the stranger went on, "he's really a wonderful fellow."

Mr. Foley smiled at the vanishing backs. He had good will enough for everyone. He didn't require reciprocation.

Tugging at the stiff necktie that he had bought yesterday from the door-to-door salesman, he strolled cheerfully on toward the bar. His smile was as much a part of him as the ruff of loose gray hair, the bristling black brows, the overhanging stomach, the big, comfortable, hump-toed shoes. It was as much a part of him as *Foley's,* as his confidence in the Kansas City Blues now that they were owned by the Yankees, as his pride in Reuben's barbecued ribs. He glanced at Reuben, hunched on a stool in the kitchen, reading the paper. Reuben had been a houseboy for one of the Swopes in his younger days. The experience had given him a taste for high society. He followed its dinners and dances and divorces with care. Mr. Foley smiled at him, but Reuben didn't notice. He was absorbed in a guest list. *Old Reuben,* Mr. Foley thought. *Old black Rube. Maybe I'll have me a plate of ribs later on when I get good and cooled off.*

At the end of the passage, Mr. Foley paused and gazed into the room. The room was full of people tonight, and, as always, they were all his friends. His interest in them was personal. They might all have been his guests: the elderly couple drinking beer at the corner table, the group of young men shouting at the bar, the hilarious crowd around the pinball machine, the dancers in the cramped space in front of the thundering juke box, the couple silently holding hands across the red-and-white-checked tablecloth, the voice up front that wanted service. Mr. Foley smiled his contentment, and plucked a peanut from a bowl on the bar. He dropped the shell on the littered floor and smiled at everyone. Mr. Foley hadn't an enemy in the world and he had never had a quarrel in his life. Nothing could hold out against the endless vitality of his happiness and his huge, unwavering smile.

The voice cried again for service, and Mr. Foley watched his daughter moving among the tables. Mona was a tall, slender girl, with a wide mouth, discontented eyes, and a pepper of freckles saddling her nose. Mr. Foley knew that she wasn't pretty, and her gravity puzzled him, but he liked having her working here. She was his only child and all that remained of Josephine. Someone spoke to Mr. Foley, but he let him go by with only a smile. He was absorbed in his daughter. Mona had paused at a small table up front and was talking to a young man with smooth black hair and a hard, bony jaw. Something in her expression and the way she held her head made Mr. Foley think of his wife.

Josephine had not lived to see *Foley's.* She had known only the dim, struggling years of the pool hall on East Thirty-First Street, the lunchroom on Troost Avenue, and the drive-in diner on Highway 50, just across the state line, in Kansas. Josephine had died, disciplined to failure, surrendered to hopelessness, six weeks after beer came back in 1933. Mr. Foley stared over Mona's distant, lowered head at the proud flash of the proud blue sign, and the smile dimmed a little on his face. He still missed Josephine, after all these years, and it troubled him that he could no longer assemble her image in his mind. He could only remember how tired she had been, and how good. But regret was foreign to Mr. Foley. Memory spent itself, and the smile came securely back. *Poor Josie,* he thought. *She sure would have scalped me for buying that cooling system.*

Mr. Foley leaned an elbow on the bar and wondered if the temperature had fallen since his last reading. But he didn't really care. He popped a peanut into his mouth and glanced along the bar. At the far end, Fred, the bartender, measured and poured and stirred. He was an elderly young man, prematurely bald, with a painful complexion and three brilliant, gold front teeth. Fred didn't drink or smoke, but he had a taste for sweets. He was partial to Hershey Kisses and there was always a sack of them somewhere under the bar. His other interest was stamps. Mr. Foley watched him slide two drinks across the bar, and feel for the hidden sack. The sight made Mr. Foley chuckle. A couple near by looked up and stared, and exchanged a private glance.

Mr. Foley continued his aimless patrol. He swung his smile this way and that, feeding his capacity for happiness on snatches of overheard conversation. Vicarious friendship satisfied him. It left him free to ruminate on nothing.

A voice at his elbow said, "So I called him up the first thing in the morning. That was Tuesday. And sure enough . . ."

"Didn't I tell you, Harry?" a woman said. "I just knew, darling."

She caught Mr. Foley's eye, coldly. He smiled and nodded. He moved on, and into a big man in a tight yellow polo jersey.

"Watch it, Mac," the man said.

"Oh," Mr. Foley said. "Excuse me. I must have—"

"Okay," the man said.

Mr. Foley sidled away, through a convulsion of laughter, and smiled as if he understood. He circled a table of boisterous youths. One of them returned one of his smiles. Mr. Foley beamed, and again caught sight of Mona. She was coming toward him, headed for the bar, swinging an empty tray. He cut between the tables to meet her.

They met at the head of the bar, but they could only smile. Somebody had turned on the radio. The voice of a news commentator stood between them.

They walked back down the bar together. The voice fell away behind them, blending with the shrill vivacity of the Andrews Sisters from the juke box.

"I looked at the temperature a minute ago," Mr. Foley said. "It—"

"What?" Mona said.

"I said I looked at the temperature," Mr. Foley said. "I was out in the garden. It's ninety-five. Think of it. Ninety-five."

"It is?" Mona said. She ran an idle finger through her thick, dark hair. "I guess that's why we've got such a crowd."

Mr. Foley looked at her anxiously.

"If you're tired," he said. "I mean, maybe I'd better—"

They both knew that it was merely a gesture. Mr. Foley's days of active service were over. He couldn't remember orders any more. His attention was always diverted by the conversation at the next table.

"No," Mona said. "I'm not tired."

"Well," Mr. Foley said. "In that case."

"I feel fine," Mona said.

Mr. Foley smiled and patted her shoulder and let her go. He scooped a handful of peanuts from one of the bowls on the bar. He wandered off toward the kitchen and back up front again. The sound of the telephone pierced the familiar clamor. Mr. Foley turned and headed for the booth. But Mona was ahead of him. He saw her vanish through the door. He shrugged, and cocked his ears again for entertainment. He loitered past a lovelorn couple and a silent man with two whispering women. Just beyond them, at a disheveled table by the wall, sat three disheveled men in white linen suits. Mr. Foley hovered and halted, and beamed.

"Everything all right, gentlemen?" he said. "Got everything you want?"

One of the men looked up, and away. He said sharply, "But that was before he sold out."

One of the others gave a grunt.

The third man said, "Sold out? What do you mean, sold out?"

"Come on, Lou," the second man said. "Forget it."

"I mean, sold out," the first man said. "I was there. I saw the son of a bitch with my own two eyes."

Mr. Foley started. He drew the line at coarse language in mixed company, and there were two middle-aged women sitting at the next table. It was impossible that they hadn't heard.

"Now, wait," the third man said. "Wait just a minute. Nobody calls Rudy Blake a son of a bitch when I'm—"

"Gentlemen," Mr. Foley said. He tapped one of the men gently on shoulder. "Gentlemen."

The man glanced up. His eyes focused slowly. He said, "Huh?"

"If you don't mind," Mr. Foley said. He smiled his warmest smile. "I know you gentlemen don't mean any harm. But if you could be just a little more careful of your language. I mean, some ladies are sitting right behind you. If you could just—"

It struck them funny. They grinned at Mr. Foley, and then twisted about in their chairs and stared at the two women. They smirked at each other and shook their heads and suddenly roared with laughter. Mr. Foley stretched his smile to its limit.

"Okay, Pop," one of them said. He fumbled for his glass. "You heard what the man said, Harve? He wants you to try and keep it clean."

His companions howled and punched each other, and leered again at the women.

Mr. Foley took a deep breath. His smile was his only diplomacy, and there had been times when it wasn't enough. He thanked his stars, and gratefully moved away. As he turned, a sudden movement caught his eye. It was the young man with the black hair he had noticed before. He had kicked back his chair and was standing rigid, staring at the three men in white. Mr. Foley stood and gaped.

The man gave a kind of jerk. It was as though something had abruptly released him. He bent over the table, and straightened up. His eyes wheeled wildly around the room. Then he thrust himself across the floor and jerked open the door and disappeared. The door twitched slowly closed.

"Well, I'll be jiggered," Mr. Foley said, and shook his head. He knew it was hopeless. *It's beyond me,* he told himself. The admission encouraged him to forget. His smile crept happily back. *He must have been sick,* he thought, and that explained it all. Mr. Foley never drank more than was good for him. But he knew what it was to overeat.

Mona Foley moved in and out among the tables, quiet, efficient, and the target of every eye. The glances followed her, blandly curious, like cattle in a field. She let them look and hardly noticed. Like the thump of the juke box and the crash of voices, they were part of her working environment.

"Two Budweisers?" she said. "And a Scotch and a bourbon?"

"Make that bourbon Old Taylor," one of the two men said. "If you've got it."

The other man said, "Wait a minute." Mona nodded, and waited, gravely. She left cordiality to her father. *Foley's* was her father's life. It was only her job. "And a pack of Luckies," the man said.

Mona moved away, aware of the two pairs of cautiously following eyes. Behind her, a woman's voice said, "Go ahead, Gene. Take a *good* look." Mona heard the tart, possessive voice with a kind of dreary anger. *You fool,* she wanted to say. The old emptiness opened in her like a weakness. She knew what Gene was looking at. She also knew he was merely looking.

As she passed down the bar, an elbow thrust suddenly out. It buried itself for an instant in the great, soft swell of her breast. The man's face remained innocently averted. It could have been an accident. But it wasn't. It had happened too many times before. Mona stepped back, and went on. She couldn't respond even with irritation. Three or four years ago, she had still been capable of annoyance. But custom honed everything down to indifference. Irritation would be an affectation now, like a blush at the sound of obscenity. She accepted the nudging arms and elbows as she had learned to accept the glances. It was hard to believe that there had ever been a time when she had sensed the latter with pride. But it had been harder to face the truth. Mona was twenty-five years old. She had been nineteen when she finally began to realize that the admiring eyes were not admiring her. None of them ever really saw Mona Foley. The eyes that had turned in the high-school corridor, that turned in the street, that were turning now from the crowded tables were only for her breasts.

Mona stepped into the bar and turned her back to the room. She could feel the stares wither and withdraw. There was nothing to nourish them in her narrow back and her narrow hips and her long, narrow legs. She got the cigarettes from the case on the back bar and opened the two bottles of beer and waited for Fred to mix the highballs. Fred never saw any part of her. She was the boss's daughter, and he didn't dare. She cracked a peanut and listlessly ate it, as if the cold emptiness were something food could fill. Up front, the juke box began to throb again, and somebody sang of love:

> *"And maybe,*
> *I'll say*
> *May be . . ."*

Mona assembled the drinks on her tray and once more faced the room. Everybody wanted her, and nobody needed her. She arched her back to defy them all and moved up the aisle between the eyes at the tables and the eyes at the bar. The commanding breasts tossed beneath the gray-green uniform blouse.

At the table, the two men fumbled and wrangled for the check. She made the change and took the tip, and the two women watched her like hawks. Mona couldn't help but envy them. They had something they wanted, something they could defend and protect. *You fools,* she thought. *You poor damn lucky fools.* Someone called and beckoned and signaled with an empty glass. It was one of the regular customers. Mona crossed to the other table. It was almost nine o'clock *Four more hours,* she thought, as if time made any difference.

"Three rum Collins," she repeated to the table. "And a Foxhead."

She would go home and read and go to bed, or Ritchie

would telephone. *Ritchie,* she thought. Somebody had introduced him to her a month ago, and he still hung on.

"Tell Fred to go easy on the sugar in those Collins," one of the men said.

"All right," Mona said.

I'll go home, she thought, and knew that Ritchie would telephone before she left. Ritchie smoked cigars and worked on the night shift at a filling station on the Country Club Plaza and he liked to have fun with her name. When he was in high spirits, he called her Moanin' Low. Ritchie had never tried to touch her, but she knew that he was only cautious. She had seen his eyes. It was impossible to believe she had once thought that he was what she wanted.

Somebody said, "Hi, Mona."

"Hello," she said, and tried to show some interest. "Can I get you something?"

"Well, now," he said. He glanced at his friends and sniggered. "I don't know—"

Mona didn't hear the rest of it. She no longer even saw him. *I'll go home,* she told herself. Home was only a book and her bed and her father stretching happily out to sleep in the other room. But she thought: *I'll go home whether he calls or not.* She had persuaded herself for almost a week that Ritchie needed something that she had to give. If he had asked, he could have had it all that first night. *Oh, God,* she thought, at the incredible memory of her willingness, her eager self-deception. The sense of guilt persisted. *But I didn't,* she told herself. *I didn't. And maybe I wouldn't have, anyway.* Ritchie's unhappiness had only been a mood. The warm rush of her sympathy, her readiness to help him as she had the others, had all been wasted again. All Ritchie had really needed was a job. The swagger reappeared at the end of his first week on the Plaza, on payday.

The juke box started up again. This time it was Glenn Miller and *Tuxedo Junction.* Filling her orders behind the bar, Mona saw her father at the dim head of the passage, staring out into the beer garden. He rose and fell slowly on his toes. His hands were clasped behind his back. He had thwarted her like Ritchie and all the others. Mona gazed at his massive contentment and remembered. He had been the first to thwart her. Driving back from the cemetery on the afternoon of her mother's funeral, she had watched him sagging like a sack in his seat, and recognized the shape of her vocation. But her father had taken her comforting hand and comforted it with his own. She remembered the shock of his gentle fingers and his tender, dismaying smile. He had thought it was she who needed affection and sympathy. He didn't know that she had been prepared to devote her life to him.

"Three rum Collins," Fred said, and deposited them on her tray. "Right?"

Mona nodded, and edged out of the bar and up the room. The elbow blocked her path again, but this time she saw it and dodged. She handed around the drinks on her tray, accepted a tip and a cautious leer, and saw the front door open. A man came gingerly in. For a moment he stood hesitant. Then he walked quickly to a small table by the wall, sat quickly down, and quickly lighted a cigarette. She went to serve him, thinking wearily of Ritchie.

Mona wondered if it would have to be Ritchie after all. She was twenty-five years old, and time went by so swiftly, so slowly. The need to give herself, to devote herself, to supply an urgent need from her boundless resources, was growing in her like a malignancy. *But, Ritchie,* she thought. The hint of satisfaction in that first fumbling effort in the Ullmans' garage had condemned her to respond only to insufficiency. Harold Ullman had walked home with her from the school library, silent and sickly and the butt of every joke, and she had been drawn to him like a magnet. His flood of gratitude on the swaybacked cot, under the dangling inner tubes and the mural of old license plates, had aroused and released and directed her. He had showed her forever the meaning of love. Love was the mother favoring the crippled child, indifferent to the rest. Love was reaching out to weakness and strengthening it with her strength. She had only to remember Harold Ullman to know that it wasn't Ritchie.

Mona paused beside the wall table. She gazed down at the dark head and the hard jaw. He didn't look up. A copy of *Time* lay open before him and he appeared to be lost in the deeps of National Affairs.

"Can I get you something?" she said.

His reaction stunned her to interest. It was as though she had shouted a warning. He went tense, like a dog on point. But it wasn't the tension of ordinary surprise. It didn't spring from abstraction. She had a curious feeling that he hadn't been reading at all. She was suddenly certain that he had known she was there, and had only been waiting for her to speak. He cautiously raised his head. His eyes dodged across her face with what could have been either fear or ferocity.

"Yes," he said. His glance darted to the next table, to the one beyond, to somebody standing at the juke box, and back. "Yes, I—" His voice was rusty from silence. He cleared his throat. "I'd like a bourbon and plain water."

"Bourbon and plain water," Mona said, and couldn't move. His strangeness held her rooted.

His eyes returned from another patrol, and narrowed. He said, "Well?"

"Oh," Mona said. "I'm sorry— You said a bourbon and plain water?"

"That's right," he said. "But I'm in kind of a hurry."

"It won't take a minute," she said.

She freed herself and backed away. Her throat felt as dry as his. It was all she could do not to look back. *What happened?* she thought, and had no idea what she meant.

"Young lady!"

It was a large man with two slim women. He waved a hairy hand.

Mona said, "Just a moment, please."

It was the least she could do. He had said he was in a hurry. *But even so,* she told herself. Even if he did. That was no kind of reason. That didn't explain— She felt her mind go limp.

A smile blocked her way. She shook her head, and recognized her father. *I'm in a hurry,* she wanted to say. But, instead, she raised an answering smile. They walked together down the aisle, away from a radio harangue. Her father said something, and nodded and smiled.

"What?" she said.

"I said I looked at the temperature," he said. "I was out in the garden. It's ninety-five. Think of it. Ninety-five."

"It is?" Mona said. She made an effort, and added, "I guess that's why we've got such a crowd."

She didn't hear his reply, but she saw the expression on his face.

"No," she said. "I'm not tired."

"Well," he said. "In that case."

"I feel fine," Mona said.

She wondered if she did. Her father dropped a genial hand on her shoulder, and genially drifted off. She turned to watch him. But she knew it wasn't he that she wanted to see. She caught a glimpse of the smooth black head. He was still there. A wave of relief rolled over her, and was suddenly dissolved in annoyance. *What is the matter with me?* she thought. *Why shouldn't he still be there?* She stepped furiously to the bar. A man on a stool instantly averted his eyes, and coughed.

"Please, Fred," she said. "I'm in a hurry."

Fred shifted a bit of chocolate on his tongue. He gave her an injured look. "You only said one," he said.

The drink was on the bar in front of her.

"Oh," she said, and laughed, at Fred, at herself, at everyone.

"What's so funny?" Fred said.

"Nothing," she said. "I don't know. I haven't the faintest idea."

Fred swallowed and licked his lips. "You better get a grip on yourself," he said.

"I know," she said.

Mona went gaily up the aisle and across the room. Over the last heads she could see him lighting a cigarette. Everyone seemed to be looking at her but him. She giggled at all the ubiquitous eyes, and wondered if this was happiness.

"There," she said. She deposited the glass on *Time*. "How's that for speed?"

"What?" he said. "Oh, sure. That was fine. Thanks very much."

Mona watched him lift the glass and drink. It was as though she had prepared it herself, as though it were something more than whisky and water. *Please,* she thought. *Please have him see me.*

She said, "Is it—all right?"

In the booth a dozen feet away, the telephone rang.

"Yes," he said. "Sure. It's fine."

He gave her an uncertain glance. The telephone rang again, and she couldn't speak. He began to feel through his pockets.

He said, "How much do I owe you?"

Mona shook her head. "No," she said. "No—you don't have to pay me now. I'll—"

She saw a kind of suspicion cloud his eyes.

"Wait," she said. The telephone was ringing and there was nothing she could do but answer it and it was sure to be Ritchie. "Wait just a minute," she said. "I'll be right back. I've got to answer the phone."

She ran frantically to the booth, and she had been right. It was Ritchie.

"Mona?"

"Just a second," she said. She reached for the door and drew it to. She couldn't have anyone hear. "Yes?"

"This is me," he said.

Through the glass panel she could see a corner of the juke box, a section of the bar, three tables. But she couldn't see the table by the wall. *I can't even see him,* she thought. She sat trapped in the booth, with Ritchie.

He said briskly, "Everything's worked out swell. I made

a deal with Max. Can you be ready a little before one?"

It was fantastic.

She said, "No."

His voice staggered. The sound gave her a twitch of pleasure. Hope swept her on to ruthlessness.

"I won't be here," she said. "I'm going to leave when Papa does."

"Well," he said. "Then suppose I—"

"No," she said.

"But I thought—"

"I want to go home," she said.

There was a heavy silence. She gazed out at the backs at the bar, and shuddered. An hour ago she might have let him come. *No, I wouldn't,* she told herself. *I'd already made up my mind. He hasn't anything to do with it at all.*

"Well," Ritchie said. "If that's the way you feel about it."

"Yes," she said. "It is." She was immediately sorry. It was as much her fault as his. "I'm sorry, Ritchie."

He gave a kind of grunt. "Okay," he said, and hung up.

Mona dropped the receiver back on its hook. She wondered if this time he meant it. But Ritchie was invulnerable. He would never withdraw in defeat. She opened the door and suddenly remembered. It was incredible. She had almost forgotten. The memory of the dark, unhappy head shook her like a memory of happiness. She flung herself out of the booth.

A young couple stood just inside the street door, gazing curiously around, as if they had expected something quite different.

Mona gave them a smile of pure delight, and turned. The table by the wall was empty.

She refused to believe it. He couldn't have gone. She had asked him to wait. It was impossible that he hadn't understood. She told herself that he had only gone back to *Men.* He couldn't have left. There wasn't any reason.

There was no hat on the rack above the chair where he had sat. But that meant nothing. She couldn't be sure that he had worn a hat. She knew he hadn't worn a hat. She was certain.

But the ice was melting in the half-finished drink on the table. A half-finished cigarette was crumpled in the ash tray. *Time* had vanished, and in its place lay a quarter, two dimes, and a nickel.

He had gone. He had really gone. Her heart turned over.

Sitting alone at a table by the wall, Leland Sessions watched the waitress disappear into the telephone booth. The telephone rang once more, and stopped. She had told him to wait. He wondered uneasily why. He looked down at his glass and then back at the booth again, and asked himself what her strange remark and her stranger behavior meant. He could only suppose that she had recognized him. It was the obvious explanation, but it left him unconvinced. He knew the look of recognition. In the long, slow, solitary weeks since June he had sensed it too many times and in too many faces not to know its manifestations. Recognition didn't mask itself in cordiality. It was cold and condemning and furtive.

The door of the telephone booth closed. Leland picked up his glass and tried to reassure himself. He had never been in *Foley's* before. He didn't know its rules and customs. Her excited hospitality might be simply a policy of the place. His mind ran back over the commonplaces of their conversation. Her manner had been strange, but there had been nothing in the least alarming in anything she had said. She had only talked. He wondered if that explained it. It had been weeks since anyone had shown any inclination to talk to him. But she hadn't lingered at any of the other tables. He didn't understand her at all. He knocked an ash from his cigarette, and thought, violently: *What of it? What difference does it make?* He beat her out of his mind. She was only one of them. The threat of the raised voice and the accusing finger was everywhere. If she had recognized him, there was nothing he could do about it now. He had to be alert for the recognition that might explode into action. There was no comfort for him in the fact that it hadn't happened yet. It would. It was bound to, sooner or later.

His eyes moved swiftly down the bar and among the clustered tables. A large man in shirt sleeves wandered here and there, smiling a prodigious, proprietary smile. That, he supposed, was Foley. He swung his gaze along the bar again. Anticipation was his only weapon. He had to be ready to act at the first intimation of danger. No one returned his glance. But when he shifted his eyes, he could feel the heads turning to stare, and the usual whispers begin. He couldn't hear what they said, but it was impossible not to know. He might have been listening at every table. At the far end of the room, a man raised his eyebrows. That was: "I thought he looked familiar." In the crowd at the bar, somebody nudged his neighbor. That could only be: "Don't look now, but . . ." A woman lowered her head and shielded her mouth with her hand. He knew what that meant, too: "Wouldn't you think he'd have the common decency to . . ." He knew them all, and they all knew him. If the waitress hadn't recognized him, she was the only one. He knew he didn't belong here, or anywhere. He carried his difference with him. It marked him off like a deformity.

Leland felt for his drink. He wondered if even his arrest would satisfy them. Kindness seemed to have gone out of the world. It appalled him to remember that he had thought this might be pleasure. He brought his glass up to his mouth and gulped down a purposeful swallow. There had been four other bars tonight, but the protective indifference had just begun to stir. He wasn't drunk yet. It was still only an eventuality. But it would come, and if not here, somewhere else. It didn't matter where. One bar was much like another, and in each new place, for a few minutes at least, he could count on a kind of anonymity. For a few minutes it was almost possible to believe that he was still like everybody else.

The large man was still roaming the room, as if he had misplaced something of no value. The man moved his head, and their eyes met. Leland swung his gaze away: to the windows, to the bar, to the juke box. Mistrust brought it slowly and carefully back. The man had halted. He was bending over three rumpled men in white. Leland watched the huge smile widen, the big hand drop intimately on a shoulder, and the three heads lift with interest. One of the men nodded and one of them smiled, and suddenly all three of them laughed. The large man smiled his monstrous smile and the men at the table shook with laughter. The sound exploded through all of the other voices, through the music, through the shuffle of feet on the dance floor.

Leland thought: *It's just a joke. It can't be anything but a joke.* He tried to hope.

The smile sagged a little on the large man's face, and then sprang heavily back into place, as if he had caught it just in time. He said something to the other three, and pointed. The three heads turned slowly around. Leland's fingers went numb on his glass. They were looking in his direction. They were staring at him—and laughing. Leland stared back at the shaking shoulders and the open mouths and the leering eyes, and sat helpless with horror. He could hold his own against the whispers and the glances. He was prepared, if necessary, even for violence. But he had never dreamed that he would have to submit to this. It was impossible that heartlessness could go so deep. But it could. It had.

The evidence blazed on the three contorted faces. They thought he was funny.

Rage abruptly released him. He kicked back his chair and stood up. Everyone could see him now, but that no longer mattered. He dared them to look. He willed them to look. The pretense of all the averted faces only fed his fury. He wanted them all to see. They had harried and hounded and bullied him long enough. But he would never run again. They had finally gone too far. He dropped his cigarette into the ash tray. He took a final sip of his drink and pushed the glass aside. He remembered the tip and put it on the table. He picked up *Time,* and turned and walked away. The door was somehow stuck. He had to wrench it open, but action was what he wanted. The door wheezed shut behind him on its patent device. He stood on the sidewalk, with the night heat soaking through his clothes like a shower of rain. He looked up at the grim blue light of the hissing neon sign and let the exultation come.

The pale moonlit sky looked down. Around the globe of the street lamp at the corner, a horde of insects swarmed and swirled like mist. *Let them laugh,* he told himself, and watched a car nose in to the curb on the other side of the street. Everything had changed. Let them all laugh if they liked. Let them all stare. Let them do their worst. They couldn't alter his innocence. He yearned to test his strength again.

He wanted another crowd to ignore. He wanted another door to wrest open. He blamed all his fears on his failure at Harrisonville and on the stammering crank on the telephone last week, and his weakness filled him with disgust. They had combined to force him into every appearance of guilt.

The car at the curb reversed a yard or two and pulled forward again, and halted. It was a large family sedan. A couple emerged, both sliding under the wheel and out the driver's side. They came across the street, hand in hand. Leland watched them: a boy and a girl in their teens, wearing smudged brown-and-white saddle shoes.

They came chattering up the sidewalk beneath the wheeling fog of insects. He stood at the door and watched them, trembling with strength and fury. The couple straggled to a stop.

"Oh," the girl said.

They had been too absorbed to notice him.

"Excuse me," the boy said.

Leland looked at them.

The boy hesitated. "Uh," he said. "Excuse us, please."
Leland said, "What?"

The eyes blinked in the two unformed faces. The boy made a doubtful sound. The clasped hands parted, self-consciously. Leland thought: *Make me move. Make me.* He stared at them. Yesterday, or even an hour ago, he would have been the one to hesitate and lower his eyes and back away.

He said, "You want to go in?"

The girl's eyes widened. "Has something happened?" she said. "I mean—"

Leland glanced from one young face to the other. He wondered if they had recognized him yet. *Take a good look at me,* he thought. *I'll give you something to talk about.*

The boy gulped, and found his voice.

He said, "Is— I mean, has there been some trouble?"

The girl said, "Buddy. Wait. If something's happened, we—"

"No," Leland said. "It's all right." It was now. He was satisfied. He stepped aside. "There's no trouble."

"Well," the boy said uneasily. "Well, thanks. We sure don't want any trouble."

Leland didn't reply. He walked away without looking back. The door opened, and closed. They would be inside now, turning excitedly to each other: "Did you see who that was?" He wondered which of them would be the first to say it. He walked slowly down the sidewalk toward his car. In the rear of a grocery store a small light burned like a spark among the shadowy shelves and counters. The anger drained slowly out of him, and a kind of shame seeped in. They had bullied him into bullying. He tried to hope that Buddy and his girl hadn't recognized him after all. He didn't want them to know that that had been Leland Sessions. He lighted a cigarette, and threw it away. He didn't want to smoke. He didn't even want another drink. The only thing he wanted was to go home and get into bed. But this time it wasn't flight. The choice was entirely his own.

He wearily challenged them all: the doubtful couple at the door, the jeering men in white, the staring waitress, the whisperers, the watchers. He supposed that this was indifference.

THREE

MONA SNAPPED OFF THE LIGHT in *Ladies* and stood for a moment in the absolute dark, thinking of Ritchie. It had been a mistake to see him again. *But what could I do?* she asked herself. He telephoned almost every night. She hadn't the courage, or the strength, to put him off every time. Ritchie's ardor wouldn't be blunted by anything short of success. She remembered last night with distaste: the aimless driving about, the drinks at the roadhouse, the usual inconclusive struggle in the apartment vestibule. But sooner or later— She pushed the thought from her mind. It was too hard a price for freedom.

She came out into the light of the corridor, holding her pocketbook under her arm, annoyed with herself, with Ritchie, with everything. *What's the matter with me?* she thought, and tried to pretend that she had forgotten the night more than a week ago. *I wouldn't even know him if I saw him again,* she told herself. It was ridiculous. But going up the corridor to the emptied barroom, she knew that it wasn't true. She would know him anywhere. The clock in the kitchen said ten minutes after twelve. Reuben was bent over the sink, holding a handful of silver under the tap. She went on to the bar. Fred was clearing the bottles off the back bar, locking the beer taps. The clatter from the kitchen and the tiny clink of the shifting bottles spoke to her of contentment. She walked listlessly through the carpet of peanut shells. Fred was only ten years older than she was, but he stood with the old Negro in the security of compromise. She felt a wave of envy—for Reuben and his kitchen and for Fred and his tidy bar. She had only the endless patrols among the tables, and Ritchie. There had to be something more. She pressed her breasts against the rim of the bar, as if they were somehow to blame. Fred turned an indifferent head.

"Papa would do the same," Mona said. "There's just no point in staying open any longer."

Fred shrugged. She was the boss's daughter. His enthusiasm was reserved for his stamp collection. Even the Hershey Kisses were just a habit.

"It's all right with me," he said.

"I know Papa won't care," she said. "Besides, we've got Friday night coming up tomorrow."

"It suits me," Fred said.

Friday was Ritchie's day off. He would spend the evening here, smoking cigars and watching her, and waiting. At one, she would follow him out to his car.

Fred bent down and came up with his candy sack. He shook it carefully. It was almost empty. He frowned.

"Well," Mona said. "I guess I'll go. I locked the back door and turned off the unit. You better fix the lights. Papa said Reuben left the sign on last night."

Fred put a chocolate in his mouth, and rolled the tinfoil wrapper into a tiny ball.

"Okay," he said, indistinctly. "I'll take care of it. That sign costs money."

Mona took up her pocketbook. "Well, good night," she said.

"Good night," Fred said. "And tell your Dad I hope his stomach ache is better."

"I will," Mona said. "I'm sure he'll be all right tomorrow. He always is."

She made her way through the barren tables. The lights went out in the back corridor and above the bar. Behind her the room dimmed and filled with shadows. She opened the door on the lonely night and the three long blocks to the car line, and stopped. There was the sound of a car roaring up from the distant Plaza. It couldn't be Ritchie. She had told him she had a cold, and was going straight home to bed. But Ritchie had his own ideas. He liked to take her by surprise. The car shot over the top of the hill. There was a howl of brakes and tires and laughter. It yawed wildly around the corner and into Forty-Ninth Street, and was gone. Mona let her breath out slowly, and looked cautiously up and down the street. The usual cars were parked for the night at the usual intervals along the silent, sleeping block. None of them was Ritchie's, with its double spotlights, its oversize tires, its panoply of projecting mirrors, its foxtail flying from the radio antenna. She moved away to cross the street—and saw him.

For an instant she didn't recognize him. He was only a man in a blue seersucker suit standing hesitant on the corner, with a magazine in his hand and a whirling halo of insects. Then he moved his head, and the movement told her who he was. She looked at him with wonder, and wondered why she wasn't surprised. But it was as if she had known it would happen. It was as if they had met like this a hundred times before. It was as if they had always met on this corner, on this night, at this hour.

It was as familiar as the empty street and the dark, damp smell of midnight. She hesitated, and then walked calmly down to meet him. It was all she could do to keep from trembling.

"Hello," she said, and smiled. "How are you tonight?"

He had been looking at her, watching her coming toward him, but he started.

He said, doubtfully, "Why—hello."

There was a pause. She hoped her smile didn't tell him everything she felt. But he wasn't looking at her. His glance had moved away. He was gazing into the window of the grocery store on the corner, at a cardboard man with a steaming cup of cardboard coffee. She tried to think of something sensible to say.

She said, "Do you live around here?"

His head jerked back.

"I?" he said. He looked at her with astonishment, and suspicion. "No—no, I don't. I live out on Aberdeen Road." He paused, as though he had asked a question. "I just stopped for a drink at that bar up there. But it looks like it's closed up already."

"Yes," Mona said. She didn't understand him at all. He was like nobody else in the world. Excitement tripped her heart. She said, "It is closed. Papa went home early and I didn't see any sense in staying open right up to the limit. We haven't had a customer for hours."

"Oh," he said, and frowned. "Papa?"

"Mr. Foley," she said. She pointed toward the pale-blue neon sign with her pocketbook. The dark, suspicious eyes followed her gesture.

It was like a signal. The sign gave a sudden flicker and faded. The color ran out like water. "He's my father," she said.

"Oh," he said.

The door opened beneath the drained sign. Reuben and Fred emerged, wearing dark jackets and identical stiff straw hats. Fred waited for the door to close, and tried the lock. He stepped back and looked up at the dark sign. Then they cut across the sidewalk and across the street, walking in step like a vaudeville team, and headed down the hill toward the car line. Mona watched them out of sight behind a jungle of shrubbery in the small, neglected yard of the vacant corner house.

"The colored one is Reuben," she said. "He's the cook. The other is the bartender. His name is Fred and he collects stamps. What do they call that? It's numis-some-thing."

"Numismatics," he said. "But that isn't stamps. Stamp collectors are philatelists. Numismatics is coins. I had a coin collection one time."

"You did?" she said. She was even interested in that. She wanted to take his arm. "Really?"

"When I was a kid," he said. "But somebody stole them —it. We reported it to the police, but—" He stopped.

"What happened?" she said.

"Nothing," he said.

She waited, but he didn't go on. He glanced at her, and then away. His silence was suddenly frightening. It had the feel of finality. But it couldn't end now. It couldn't end like this.

She said, as if that explained everything, "You don't remember me."

"Yes, I do," he said. He looked at her with a kind of relief. "I didn't at first. But I remember you now."

"I had on my uniform before," she said. "That makes a difference."

"Yes," he said. "I suppose it does."

"I hate the darn thing," she said. "I hate everything about it. I picked it out myself and it's really very attractive." She smiled. "But you know what I mean."

He nodded, vaguely. It was obvious that he had no idea what she meant. He felt through his pockets and brought out a cigarette and struck a match. The flame flared like a beacon in the warm, unmoving air. He dropped the match at his feet. "Well," he said.

She said, "My name is Mona."

He raised his head. He started to speak, and didn't. His face gave a twitch and hardened.

"What?" she said.

"Nothing," he said. "I didn't say anything."

"I thought you were going to say something," she said. He looked at the cardboard man in the window.

"Yes," he said. "I was. I was going to tell you my name." He looked at her abruptly. "But I guess you know it."

"No," she said. She stared at him in surprise. "After all," she said, and giggled, "we've never been introduced. I—" The look on his face made her stop. She said in alarm, "What's the matter?"

"You don't know my name?" he said. "You don't know who I am?"

"Why, no," she said. "What's the matter?"

"Oh," he said. "I see."

"I don't understand," she said. "I—"

He said, with a kind of anger, "My name is Sessions." It might have been a threat. "Leland Sessions."

"Oh," she said. The name had a familiar sound, like the name of a long-forgotten schoolmate. Then, all at once, she remembered. It had been in all the papers two or three months ago. There had been a murder in his house. The maid had been stabbed to death in her room and he had been questioned by the police and for a few days the papers had hinted. She stared at him. Was it possible? He looked as if he could. He looked as if he could do anything. A kind of spasm ran through her. She felt her nipples rise and stiffen. But he hadn't. She knew he hadn't. Everybody knew he hadn't. She had heard the talk at the tables and the bar. After the first few days, everybody agreed that he couldn't have. But it wouldn't make any difference if he had. Nothing could make any difference.

He said, "You know who I am now. You know now, don't you?"

"Yes," Mona said. "I know who you are. I remember seeing your name in the paper. I guess I saw your picture, too."

"That's right," he said, and dropped his cigarette to the sidewalk. He ground it carefully out with his toe. "I thought so," he said. "I thought you would."

He kicked the mangled butt away, and she had a sudden picture of the cigarette smoldering in the green glass ash tray, the abandoned drink, the money left on the table.

She said in alarm, "Where are you going?"

"Why?" he said.

But it wasn't going to happen that way again. Ritchie couldn't interrupt this time. She wasn't bound to her tables tonight. It couldn't end now. This was the beginning.

"I thought you wanted a drink," she said. "Don't you want a drink? A bourbon and plain water. That's what you like, isn't it?"

He looked at her blankly. He might not even have heard. She said, "Don't you want a drink?"

"Yes," he said. "Sure. But—your place is closed."

She wanted to throw her arms around him. It was all right again. She had been right. She had known. She knew she was smiling idiotically.

"I know," she said. "But I know lots of other places. After all, I'm in the business." She slipped her arm through his. "I'm a wonderful guide."

FOUR

A WOMAN IN A LAVENDER BLOUSE AND JADE EARRINGS emerged from the telephone booth. She walked slowly back to the bar, smiling a hangdog smile. The bartender dropped another cube of ice into her drink, and raised his eyebrows. She shook her head.

"Tough," the bartender said.

"I couldn't care less," the woman said. "But I don't understand why he didn't leave any word. Are you real sure he didn't say anything?"

The bartender gave the bar a swipe with his cloth.

"Not to me, he didn't," he said.

"I just can't understand it," she said.

At the end of the room, the waiter leaned against the wall, rubbing a raw, hay-fevered nose. Mona shook the ice in her glass. She smiled at Leland in the bar mirror. He gripped his glass and watched her, as if only his gaze could keep her here, as if she might slide off the stool at any minute and disappear. The look told her everything. She could have laughed or sung or cried.

"Bourbon and plain water," she said to his image in the mirror. The words might have held a secret meaning that had just been revealed to her. "I don't think I've ever had whisky with plain water before. I know I haven't. That's funny, isn't it?"

"Yes," he said, and gazed gravely at her grave, gray eyes.

"It's a wonderful drink," she said. The bartender gave her a dubious glance, and yawned. She took another swallow that she couldn't taste. "Let's have another one," she said. "And when we finish that, we'll have another."

"Sure," he said. "Why not? But—" He shrugged and shook his head, as if the thought were too complex to put easily into words.

"What?" she said. She wanted to know everything that crossed his mind. She had to know. It was imperative.

"I don't know," he said. "I mean, when I left home to-night, I never expected—"

"I know," she said. "I know." She thought: *If Papa hadn't got sick. That's awful. But it's true.* She added, "Me, too."

He nodded, and moved his glass back and forth on the polished wood. He needed a shave and a flake of cigarette paper had stuck to his lower lip and the knot of his necktie was dark with sweat. But the restlessness had faded from his eyes and they didn't move from her face. An hour ago, as they had come through the door and crossed the room to the bar, he had looked once at the bartender and once at the waiter and once at the woman in the lavender blouse. Then he had fixed his gaze on the mirror, and on her. *That was when he saw me,* Mona thought. *He didn't really see me before. Not even in the car.* She watched him lift his glass and drink.

He said, slowly, "I feel like somebody else."

"We are," she said. She didn't know what he meant, or what she meant. But it didn't matter. The sense of urgency gave way. There was no hurry. There was plenty of time. This was all she really wanted now. It was enough that they were together. It was enough to know that it had really happened.

"It's wonderful," she said, and emptied her glass at a gulp. "Isn't it wonderful?"

"Yes," he said.

"And we'll have lots more drinks," she said. "I'll be tight and I've only been tight once before in my life. But we will, won't we? We'll have lots and lots and lots."

"Yes," he said.

At the end of the room, the waiter gave a strangled cry. He took a lurching step and stiffened and sneezed. He leaned back against the wall and buried his face in a handkerchief.

"You know something?" the woman in the lavender blouse said. "I've got a good mind to just go home."

"Tomorrow is Friday," Mona said, and thought of Ritchie. "But I don't even care."

Leland nodded, as if he understood.

The bartender looked at the clock. He trudged up the bar, clearing his throat. "Closing up, folks," he said. "They been on us lately."

"Now?" Leland said. "You mean, right now?"

Mona said, "It isn't time. Why, it's only—"

The bartender picked up their empty glasses. "They been clamping down on us for a month now." He looked at Leland. "That'll be a dollar eighty."

"But we just got here," Mona said. It seemed only a minute ago. "We wanted another drink."

The bartender punched the cash register. With his back to them, he said, "I would if I could, folks. But the law says one-thirty. The law and the boss both. They been clamping down on us lately."

The waiter came slumping up from the back of the room and leaned an elbow on the bar.

The woman in the lavender blouse said, "Maybe I ought to try just once more."

"Huh?" the waiter said.

"I wasn't addressing you," she said.

She drifted unsteadily away.

Leland put his change in his pocket. "Well," he said. "I guess that's that."

"Never mind," Mona said. It was the way it had been on the sidewalk in front of the grocery store. *It can't end now,* she told herself. *I won't let it.* "It doesn't matter," she said. "We'll find another place."

Leland didn't reply. He held the door, and followed her out. But when they reached the sidewalk, he said, "You don't want to go home? You really want to try and find some other place?"

"Don't you want to?" she said.

"Sure," he said. They walked down the sidewalk to his car. He made a move to take her arm, and didn't. Instead, he felt for a cigarette. "Sure," he said. "I would. But I thought maybe you—"

"No," Mona said. "I want to have lots more drinks." She slipped quickly into the seat. He walked around behind the car to the other side. She welcomed him back with a smile. "We're going to have fun," she said, and wanted to move close beside him. "Aren't we?"

"I guess," he said. "I want to do anything you want to do."

She almost told him that this was enough. This was everything. She would have been willing to sit forever in this dark car on this dark street in this warm, dark, secret night.

But she only said, "I don't want to go home. Not for hours."

"Home," he said, and slammed the door. "No. I don't want to go home."

"It's a wonderful night," she said. "Isn't it a wonderful night?" She lay back in the seat and closed her eyes. "It's even almost cool."

"Yes," he said. "It is—wonderful."

"And everybody in the world is asleep," she said. "Everybody but us. They're all missing this wonderful—"

He gave a kind of snort.

It shook her erect and staring. She stared at his face in the treacherous dusk. It was tight and hard and his eyes were cold.

"To hell with them," he said. "Every damn one of them."

She put out a hand, and brought it helplessly back. Peace had ripped away. They were back once more at the beginning: at the table by the wall, under the street lamp on the corner. *I don't understand,* she told herself. *Everything I say is wrong. But I don't know why. I don't know what it is. I don't understand. Except that it isn't me. I know it isn't me. It's only what I say.*

She said, with care, "I didn't mean I was sorry. I only meant I was glad." She cautiously smiled. "I don't want anybody to be awake but us." She searched his face for reassurance, and found it. She said, recklessly, "I meant—to hell with them, too."

He said in a queer voice, "You don't mean that? You don't feel that way—too? You couldn't."

"But I do," she said. "That's exactly the way I feel."

"No," he said. "You couldn't. But—" His mouth gave a sudden twitch, and she hardly knew him. She had never seen him smile before. He turned and kicked the engine explosively alive.

"Yes," she said again. "I do."

It was more than the truth. It was a promise. She had an awful sense of finality. There was no going back now. They were committed. For an instant it was almost frightening. Certainty could be as shattering as doubt.

"I feel cold," she said. It wasn't what she meant at all.

"Cold?" he said.

She said in confusion, "No. Not really. I—"

"You couldn't be cold," he said.

"I didn't mean cold," she said. "I don't know what I meant. I just feel—" Happiness took her by surprise. She leaned against the door, weak with it. "It's just that everything is so wonderful."

His smile sank gravely out of sight. "I know," he said. "I never thought there was anybody else in the world. It's hard to believe." He shook himself. "We need another drink."

"Yes," she said.

"You still want to go somewhere?" he said. "I mean, you haven't changed your mind?"

"No," she said. "I still want to go anywhere."

He threw his cigarette away.

"Well," he said, and touched the accelerator with his toe. The engine gave an answering growl. "But where? What do you suggest?"

"I don't know," she said. "It must be almost two."

"The County?" he said. "There's a big place out toward Dodson called the Sunflower. I haven't been out there since—for quite a while. But they used to stay open all night."

"Yes," Mona said. She thought of last night and Ritchie. "They still do."

"Well, what do you think?" he said.

The Sunflower was Ritchie's favorite. The Sunflower was last night. The Sunflower was an oil-grained hand inching around her back on the dance floor, reaching for her breast. But that was last night. That was Ritchie. The weight of happiness pressed her against the door. Tonight it wouldn't be that Sunflower. It would be something as new as the future.

"The Sunflower would be wonderful," she said.

He jiggled the gear, and hesitated. "I don't suppose there will be much of a crowd," he said.

"We won't even see them," she said.

"No," he said.

He stamped abruptly on the accelerator. They shot away from the curb. The sleeping houses and the dusty trees surged up and past and away. Mona leaned against the door and watched the empty blocks reel endlessly on and on. Neither of them spoke. There was nothing more to say. It was as though the pulse of motion and the warm rush of air at the windows told them everything they needed to know. The wastes and billboards of the city limits loomed drearily up ahead. A streetcar stood abandoned in a blaze of light on a siding. In front of a tool shed a man lay sprawled on a bench, with a newspaper over his face.

The vacant lots gave way to fields. There was a smell of damp, and from a hidden pond a choir of bullfrogs moaned. Then the darkened cut-rate filling stations began and the deserted lean-to produce stands. A wandering searchlight pierced the sky.

"Here we are," Leland said. He made a dubious sound. "It looks pretty crowded. I wonder if—"

"We'll find a place all right," Mona said.

"Okay," he said.

They lurched over a ditch and across a rutted plain and up to a ragged rank of parked cars. An attendant welcomed them with a stare. The Sunflower was long and low and rambling. It was painted white and the eaves were strung with colored lights. Over the entrance hung a purple neon flower. They got out and picked their way among the ruts toward a thunder of voices and stamping feet and a far-away murmur of music.

"The last time I was here—"

He didn't go on. Instead, he dodged ahead and opened the door. He followed her into a cavernous dusk of faint blue light and seething smoke. Everybody was dancing. They twisted through the littered tables and abandoned chairs. Mona walked quickly, leading the way, with her pocketbook tight under her arm. She tried not to think of last night.

A waiter appeared. He was an elderly man with a long gray face and a plastic sunflower boutonniere. He led them to a table in the lee of the kitchen door. There was a smear of tomato sauce on a corner of the cloth and the ash tray was choked with cigarette butts and olive pits and scraps of celery. The waiter picked up the ash tray, revealing a penciled problem in multiplication, and emptied it on the floor. He helped Mona into her chair, and smiled.

"Two bourbons and plain water," Leland said.

"Yes, sir," the waiter said. "Something to go with it, maybe? A nice steak sandwich?"

Mona shook her head.

"No," Leland said. "Just the drinks." He glanced around the room, and set his jaw. "And hurry it up, if you can."

"Right away," the waiter said.

He hobbled off through the gloom.

"I didn't know we were in a hurry," Mona said.

"No," Leland said. He looked at her and smiled. "But I want a drink."

"So do I," she said, and held his smile. "But we have the whole rest of the night, haven't we? I don't feel as if I'd had a thing."

"Sure," he said, and glanced warily around the room again. "Of course."

The music expired in a wail of clarinets. There was a scatter of applause and whistles, and the dancers jostled back to their tables. A few more lights came on. The waiter returned with a loaded tray.

"That was two bourbons," he said. He put two glasses on the table and wiped his hand on the seat of his trousers. "Now, a little something to eat, maybe? A nice steak sandwich?"

"No," Leland said. "But you can bring us another round while you're at it."

"Two bourbons," the waiter said. "Right away."

Leland picked up his glass, and put it down. There was a crust of lipstick on the rim. He turned the glass around. "This is really a dump," he said. He took a long drink. "I'd forgotten. I'm sorry."

"I know," she said. "But I don't mind. I mean, unless you do." She felt a touch of panic. "You don't want to leave?"

"We just ordered another drink," he said. "Besides, there isn't anywhere else to go. Except home."

"No," she said. She took a swallow from her glass, and watched him feeling through his pockets. She said, contentedly, "Leland."

He tossed a package of cigarettes onto the table. "I don't mind a little lipstick," he said. He raised his head and smiled.

"Leland," she said.

"Lee," he said. "Nobody calls me Leland. Except my mother." He shook a cigarette loose from the package.

"And the newspapers."

"Lee," she said. She rolled it softly on her tongue. "Lee."

"What?" he said.

"Nothing," she said. "I just wanted to hear how it sounds. It's a wonderful name."

"Drink your drink," he said. "Here comes our waiter. I'm going to order another round."

There was a crash of drums, and the lights went out. A spotlight blazed around the room. It came to rest on a microphone and a rat-faced man with hair the color of shellac. He had on white flannel trousers and a green gabardine jacket that hung almost to his knees.

"Yeah, gang," he shouted.

He raised his hands above his head and howled. Somebody whistled. A shudder of sound ran through the orchestra. The master of ceremonies lowered his hands and discarded his smile. He began to sing. It was *God Bless America,* with gestures: a hand placed over the heart, the arms outstretched, an awkward salute. The orchestra accompanied him, protectively. There was a rattle of applause from the bar and the waiters. He bowed and waved and jerked his head.

Mona glanced at Leland. He sat slumped in his chair with his hand around his glass. He gave her a gloomy smile.

"Direct from the East," the master of ceremonies cried.

A trumpet sounded the opening bars of *Bugle Call Rag.* Another spotlight went on. A girl in white shorts, a red blouse, and a blue shako scampered out onto the floor and blew a kiss to the master of ceremonies. He whooped and vanished. She plunged into a military tap. At the far end of the room somebody raised his head from the table, blinked heavily around, and slumped back to sleep again. A man edged out of the rest room and halted with a look of bewilderment, as though he didn't recognize the place.

The show went on and on. A girl in a domino mask bared her breasts in a pale-green light. The master of ceremonies sang again, and told a salacious story full of famous names. Two young Negroes danced with their ankles chained together. The tap dancer returned in a grass skirt and writhed to a lugubrious guitar. It was impossible to ignore the spendthrift energy. Mona had seen it all before, but it held her like a spell. It ended in a bedlam of song and screams and somersaults.

The musicians stood up and stretched. Somebody passed around a bottle. The guitarist struck a chord. A trumpet called and a trombone bayed. At the piano, a fat little man stabbed at the keys with his fat little fingers, and bobbed his head and grinned. Everybody trooped back to the dance floor. The rafters rang with *One O'Clock Jump.*

"Oh, Lee," Mona said. "I love that. Dance with me."

He gave her a startled look.

"Dance?" he said. "Good Lord, I haven't danced for—" He glanced uneasily at the bobbing dancing heads. "You're not serious?"

"Yes," she said. "Please."

"I'm not very good," he said.

"You're probably wonderful," Mona said. But she didn't really care. It wasn't the music. It wasn't even that she wanted to dance. She only wanted to hold him in her arms. "So please."

"All right," Leland said. He rose abruptly to his feet. "Why not?"

He led her down to the floor with a challenging scowl. A crevice appeared in the crowd. They fought their way in, and the current thrust them off and away. Everybody looked damp and hot and determinedly drunk. The master of ceremonies bounced by in his long green coat. A fist or an elbow caught her in the small of the back. Leland had been right. He had told her no more than the truth. He danced like a man on parade, standing straight and tense, and holding her just out of reach. Not even her breasts could touch him. The other couples swooped and swerved and all but embraced. She tried to draw closer, and stumbled.

"I'm sorry," she said.

"You should be," Leland said. "I told you I was pretty bad."

"No," Mona said. She rushed to his defense. "That isn't true." It wasn't what she wanted, but it was enough. His arm was around her and her hair was brushing his cheek. It was the closest they had been. She said, "I love dancing with you."

"I started too young," he said. "My mother sent me to dancing school at ten. I guess that's why I never learned."

"I don't know how I learned," Mona said. It was as though she had always known how. Everybody had always wanted to dance with her. That had been her only real popularity. She had walked home from school alone, or with another girl. She moved remotely back and forth to his faltering lead, and remembered a hundred panting, contorted partners. "It just happened," she said.

Two whispering girls trotted past together, and Leland stepped on her toe.

"I'm sorry," he said. "Look. Don't you think—"

Mona didn't reply. She hadn't heard him. Ritchie was smiling at her coldly from a table hardly six feet away. He took his cigar from his mouth and nodded. At the table with him were two swarthy men in sport shirts and a woman in a dirty white turban. Leland swung her around, and back again. Ritchie gazed at her. She was almost close enough now to touch him.

"Congratulations," he said. "You must be feeling better."

"I am," she said, and looked away.

Leland said, "What?"

"Let's sit down," Mona said. "I don't—"

"I'm awfully sorry," Leland said. "I hurt your foot, didn't I?"

"No," she said. "I'm fine. I'm perfectly all right. I just don't feel like dancing any more. It's too hot and crowded."

She pulled him after her through the crowd. She wouldn't look back. She couldn't bear to see Ritchie sitting there with his cigar and his jealousy and his knowledge that she had lied. *Oh, damn him,* she thought. *I don't care. I don't even know him any more. But damn him anyway.*

They found their table. Leland helped her into her chair and sat down and mopped his brow.

"I'm really sorry," he said. "I wish—"

She said, shortly, "Don't be silly. It wasn't that at all. I love dancing with you." Embarrassment carried her on. "You're a wonderful dancer. I'm just tired. It's all these people—and the noise."

"Let them look," Leland said. He picked up his drink. "They don't bother me any more. I'm glad we came."

"Yes," Mona said. From across the room Ritchie was watching her grimly. She turned away from the ridiculous mustache and the clenched cigar. "But I don't like it any more. Let's go. I want to get away from them."

"Good," he said. He pushed his glass aside, as though it stood in his way. "I'm ready—just let me find that waiter."

His eagerness justified everything. He knew what she wanted. The need was in them both. Ritchie fell out of her mind like a stone. She opened her bag and smiled at her face, and waited. When he pulled back her chair, she caught his hand. It was as natural as meeting him on the corner, and as right. At the door, she thought she felt his fingers tighten on her own.

They came out into the parking lot, and incredibly it was morning. An invisible light washed everything with color. The grass had never been so green. The unpainted produce sheds were as bright and clean as silver. The highway was white and the sky was pink and the air was as cool as water. Mona clung to his hand, and thought: *I love him. I'm in love with him.* It seemed inadequate. *Love,* she thought, and the word explained nothing. She felt too solemn for the gaiety of love.

FIVE

CHARLOTTE STREET WAS FULL OF LISTLESS LIFE. Up and down the block, the families relaxed on the little apartment balconies among the scattered Sunday papers, dull with heat and overeating. An elderly couple plodded along the sidewalk, airing a swollen dog. A Negro janitor sat in an area entrance and argued with himself in a low, complaining voice. At the curb, a young man in a sleeveless shirt was polishing a yellow coupé. A family group stood smiling grimly in the sun while somebody aimed a camera.

Anyone would have known it was Sunday. The sun poured down and the asphalt melted in the street and the radios moaned with organ music. Leland got out of his car, and set his face against the curiosity from the balconies. He walked quickly up the short walk in his new Panama hat and his starched seersucker suit to the dusty brick building where the Foleys lived. Every stare strengthened his defenses. This was the first time he had been here in the daytime since that Friday dawn a week ago, but he no longer needed darkness. It was possible to stare down any stare. He was finally armed and armored against them all. He wasn't alone any more. He had a friend.

Leland pressed the bell on the mailbox in the imitation-marble vestibule, and climbed the eroded steps to the second floor. He wondered if he would have to meet Mr. Foley. The big smiling face reared up in his mind. It had been possible to avoid him all the other times. But this was Sunday afternoon. He was almost certain to be at home today. Leland gazed at the numbered door. He braced himself with contempt, and knocked.

The door fell away from his fist. A damp, pink face beamed out at him, and a damp, pink hand caught his arm. It hauled him heartily into an overstuffed living-room.

"Well, well," Mr. Foley said. "Come right in, young man." He rubbed his hands expectantly, as if he had something to sell. "I've certainly been hearing a lot about you. Yes, indeed." He began to pump Leland's hand. "I'm mighty pleased to make your acquaintance."

"Thank you," Leland said. "I—"

"That's fine," Mr. Foley said. "Let me take your hat." He turned his head and raised his voice. "Mona! Your company's here." He laughed wildly.

Leland disengaged his hand. He backed away toward a green plush sofa. An enormous electric fan swung back and forth in a corner, grinding and clattering and slashing the heavy air. Above it a wolf crouched on a framed white hilltop, surveying a snowbound village. The sun pierced a crack in a green windowshade and dust motes reeled in the thin bright shaft of light.

"Just make yourself comfortable," Mr. Foley said. "We don't stand on ceremony here."

Leland sat down on the sofa. So this was her father. He fingered the brim of his hat and tried to conceal his distaste.

Mr. Foley dropped into a great green plush chair and tugged at the knees of his trousers. He had on a wrinkled gray shirt with the collar folded under the neckband. A flake of egg yolk was dried in a corner of his mouth.

"Mona will be right out," he said. "She's just fixing up." His big stomach heaved with amusement in the chair. "You know how women are."

Leland nodded, and waited.

Mr. Foley crossed his legs, and panted, and spoke of the weather. He talked on and on. He seemed to have no idea what he was saying. It was as if he were afraid to stop, as if he were afraid of silence.

Leland had nothing to say. This was the man and that was the smile that had turned those three men in their chairs and released their leers and laughter. He looked down at the floor. There was no escape from the voice of hypocrisy, but he was free to avoid its smile.

"Yes, sir," Mr. Foley said. "Mrs. Foley passed on seven years ago last spring. In May." Somewhere a baby began to cry. It might have been in the next room. Mr. Foley sighed and smiled. "We were raised on the same block," he said. "Mrs. Foley and I. That was up in St. Joseph. St. Joe, they call it down here. But—"

He broke off.

Mona's voice said, "Hello."

She came into the room with a faint, grave smile, wearing a crisp white dress that looked like a coat. She carried a brown pocketbook and a brown straw hat with a long white ribbon.

Leland stood up without speaking, full of the sight of her. It always surprised him. *She's lovely,* he thought. *She's really lovely.* He had no picture of her when he was alone. He could only remember her warmth and her gravity.

"Well, well, well," Mr. Foley said. He struggled up from his chair. "Don't you look nice." His smile covered them both, like a pistol.

Mona gave him a dutiful glance. She turned to Leland. "Do you mind if I don't wear a hat? I'll take it along, but I won't wear it. I don't like hats."

"No," Leland said. "Of course not." He told himself that he had never seen anything as lovely as her slow, long-legged walk. "I feel the same way. I mean, I don't like them either. But I've got a new one." He held it out, ignoring Mr. Foley. "My mother brought it home from somewhere the other day."

"Put it on," Mona said. "I want to see. Oh—I think it's terribly good-looking."

"Yes, indeed," Mr. Foley said. "It certainly is. It looks

like a genuine Panama, too."

Leland removed the hat and held it in his hand. The electric fan ground and clattered. "Well," he said. He put the hat back on his head. "I guess we'd better get—"

"Yes," Mona said, and took his arm.

Mr. Foley followed them tenaciously to the door. He gripped Leland's hand again. "It certainly has been a pleasure to make your acquaintance," he said. "Yes, indeed." Leland could hear him breathing. "Take good care of my little girl." He chuckled. "You hear?"

"Thank you," Leland said. "I will."

"Good-by, Papa," Mona said, and gently closed the door on his smile.

"Thank God," Leland said.

"Shhh," Mona said. She drew him down the hall to the steps, and stopped. "Lee," she said. "Oh—Lee."

"What?' he said.

"Kiss me," she said.

"Here?" he said.

"Yes," she said. Her fingers dug into the flesh of his wrist. "Here. Right now."

From somewhere below, something cracked like a whip. A voice cried, "It's a long fly to deep left and Di Maggio's coming in under it." There was a swell of distant cheering.

"You taste like raspberries," Leland said.

Mona rubbed her cheek against his chin, and giggled. "Like the ten-cent store, you mean," she said.

She took his arm again. She held it tightly all the way down the stairs and through the vestibule. But at the door, she took her hand away. Their intimacy was their own. They walked sedately down the sidewalk, side by side, to the car.

Mona said, "Where are we going?"

"I don't know," Leland said. He had thought no further than this. "Where would you like to go?"

"Anywhere," she said. "No—I know, Lee. I've wanted to go all summer."

"Where?" he said.

"Fairyland Park," she said.

"Oh," Leland said, and stared through the windshield at the man at work on the yellow coupé. He saw the Sunday crowds shoving their way around and around the midway of the amusement park. He saw recognition in a thousand alien faces. His stomach clenched like a fist.

"If you'd rather not," Mona said. "It doesn't really make any difference. I just—"

"No," he said. "I'd like to." His stomach tightened again. But it wasn't fear this time. He recognized a challenge. A kind of excitement shook him. "Here," he said. He pulled his hat from his head and sailed it into her lap. "Hold this, will you? Or do something with it. We're on our way. Fairyland is a dandy idea."

"Such a beautiful hat," Mona said. She moved closer to him on the seat. "But I'll put it back here on the shelf with mine. Nobody wants a hat at Fairyland Park. We'll have a wonderful time. It's been ages. I want to do everything."

"We will," he said, and wet his lips. The taste of raspberries came back. "We'll do everything there is."

He awakened the engine with a kind of fury. The tires sang around the first corner and into the quiet side street. He drove through the rambling Sunday traffic as fast as he dared.

Haste possessed him. He could hardly wait to face the first glance, and watch it wither and collapse.

"Lee," Mona said. "You're making the most awful— Is something wrong?"

He smiled at her, and touched the horn. A sedan with a back seat full of wrestling children scurried for the curb. He shook his head.

"Tell me?" she said.

He could feel the warmth of her thigh through the thin seersucker of his trousers. It might have been the source of his strength. He blew the horn again, at nothing.

"Nothing," he said. Elation hardened his jaw. "Only I wish it were dark. So I could kiss you."

"You can kiss me now," Mona said. "You can kiss me any time."

"No," he said. They were almost there. He didn't know whether he was frowning or smiling. "Not now. I don't believe in that on Sunday afternoon on Meyer Boulevard."

"I do," Mona said. "But there's always the Tunnel of Love. We could go there the very first thing."

It was some sort of Day at the park. An exhausted banner drooped above the entrance gate: *Welcome A. G. of A.* Just inside the gate, between the first hot-dog stand and the first fortuneteller's booth, the crowd caught them up. They stumbled helplessly along toward the dance pavilion. Everyone wore a bright-red badge and a bright-red papier-maché overseas cap. A company marching arm and arm bored this way and that, shouting unfamiliar words to some familiar tune. Somebody spilled a bottle of root beer on Leland's sleeve.

They lurched through the jabbing elbows and the reek of sweat, over the discarded soda bottles and the scattered popcorn, under a numbing sun and a cloud of confetti and the wail of a distant calliope. Overhead, the Big Dipper flashed like a comet, and fell with a cyclone of shrieks. Mona clutched his hand and laughed and tried to speak. He shook his head. Two racing children broke between them. The crowd threw them apart. They struggled back together. It was like trying to run in a nightmare. Leland lowered his shoulder, and shoved. A cordon of marchers snapped like a string. He reached for Mona and caught her elbow and hauled her through. They tottered into an eddy in front of the Fun House. They stared at each other, and panted.

"Are you all right?" he said.

"I guess so," Mona said, and stumbled. "I stepped on somebody's gum."

"Good God," he said. "What is all this, do you suppose?"

"There," Mona said. "I got it off. I left it for somebody else."

"Good," he said, and laughed. It was impossible to be

angry. "Just so it isn't me."

"Lee," she said. "Look where we are. I love the Fun House. It's my favorite. And it doesn't even look crowded."

But it was. A horde of caps and badges swooped up from somewhere and spun them down the entrance runway. Something hissed and somebody screamed. A jet of compressed air spurted from a hole in the floor. Mona clutched at her skirt—too late. Leland had a glimpse of long bare legs. Three boys in blue jeans snickered. They all collapsed together in a huge revolving barrel. Mona's skirt flew up to her hips again. An attendant in a white yachting cap darted eagerly in, and helped her slowly up and out. Leland emerged with a stagger and a jump.

"Isn't it wonderful," Mona said. "Oh, Lee—I'm having such a wonderful time."

The attendant stood and stared.

Leland nodded. He didn't know whether the man was looking at him or at her. But it didn't matter. He fixed him with a glare. The attendant cleared his throat and blinked his eyes. His gaze wandered off toward the barrel.

"Me, too," Leland said. It was the truth. His trousers were dirty and he was out of breath, but he had proved himself again. He could come and go as he pleased. "This is fun."

He felt for her hand and headed down a passage. Behind them the attendant dived back into the barrel to rescue a girl in a tight, transparent blouse.

Mona said, "Lee—look at yourself."

The passage was lined with panels of distorting mirrors. They stared at their grotesques: the great breasts ballooned on the squat, plump body and the seersucker suit stretched like rubber beneath the long, smudged hatchet face.

"You know," Leland said. "You should never wear white with a figure like that."

"Smile for me," Mona said. "I want to see what happens." She went limp with hilarity. "Don't—stop it. Poor Lee. You used to be so handsome."

They followed the winding passage. It brought them out at the foot of a ladder that led up to a giant slide. Mona put a hand on the guide rail, and a stab of electric current opened her mouth in a shriek. A hot sliver of air shot up Leland's leg like a snake. He pushed her ahead of him up the steep steps, and crouched behind her on a piece of sacking. An attendant gave them a shove. They plunged down the slope and over a rise and out into space, and sprawled in a heap against a padded wall, with her pocketbook spewed open and keys and compact and lipstick and cigarettes and handkerchief and coin purse and comb scattered under everybody's feet. They knelt in the dust and gazed at each other, and peacefully picked everything up.

On the midway, the crowd surged tirelessly around and around, singing and shouting and sweating. It welcomed them back with a kick in the shins and shouldered them along a placarded wall. Mona tried to comb her hair.

"Hang on to me," Leland said, and somebody sneezed in his face.

"You're all sticky," Mona said. "There's something sticky all over your coat."

"It's only root beer," he said. "I think."

"I don't like root beer," she said. "Let's pretend it's Coke."

There was a contest going on in the dance pavilion. They could see the ankles kicking along the floor at the top of the wall. They struggled through a wave of cheers and whistles. Beyond the pavilion, the crowd thinned out a trifle. They walked side by side past the shooting galleries and the baseball pitches and the ring throws and the wheels of fortune and the bingo games and the Penny Arcade. Leland lighted a cigarette.

"Win me something," Mona said. "Win me that ham. That big one there with the blue ribbon on it."

"I never won anything in my life," he said.

"You never had me before," she said. "I'll bring you luck."

"We'll see," he said, and put a dime on a checkerboard counter.

"I'm your luck," she said.

The pitchman shouted and slapped the counter with a cane and pointed to the ribboned ham, and covertly counted the dimes on the board.

"Aren't I your luck?" Mona said.

"Yes."

"All in," the pitchman shouted. "All in." He raised a hand to the numbered wheel. "All in, folks."

"I've got my fingers crossed," Mona said. "It's the biggest ham in the world. If we win, we'll have to—"

"Number nineteen," the pitchman said. "Number nineteen the winner." He raked in the dimes with a crook of his cane. Nobody had number nineteen.

"Well," Leland said.

They walked past an alley that led to the public lavatories. Beyond it was a refreshment stand in the shape of an igloo.

"He cheated," Mona said. "They always cheat. I'm still your luck."

"I know you are," Leland said. He stopped in front of the igloo stand. "How about something to drink? I'm thirsty."

"It must have been that ham," she said. "Ham always makes you thirsty. I'd love a Coke."

Leland fought his way up to the counter, and out again. Mona waved to him from a dusty bench in the shade of a dusty tree. He dodged across the walk with his two dripping trophies, and dropped down beside her.

"They didn't have any straws," he said.

"That's all right," Mona said. "At least, it's cold. Golly, I'm tired. We've hardly done anything yet and I'm ready to drop."

"We'll sit here for a while," Leland said. He was empty of everything but contentment. "But that's no way to drink out of a bottle. You have to let some air in. Didn't you ever take physics in school?"

"I guess so," she said. "But I don't remember anything about drinking out of a bottle. I'm not really tired, Lee. Just a little. I've never had so much fun."

"That's okay," he said. "We've got plenty of time. But look—do it like this. See?"

"You're wonderful," she said. "I admire you. I don't know how I ever got along without you. But you need me, too. Don't you? For luck?"

"Yes," he said, and smiled. "You're my luck, all right."

"I mean really," she said. "I know I am. Ever since that first night."

"Yes," he said.

From the direction of the dance pavilion came a sound of cheers and stomping feet. A monstrous voice boomed out: "Your attention, please. May I *please* have your attention . . ." The cheering went on. Two couples emerged from the lavatory alley and broke into a frantic trot. One of the women had a giant red vase in her arms. She gave a yelp of dismay.

"I told you," she cried. "Now we've missed it. I told you we would. We've missed the whole thing . . ."

Leland watched them twisting through the crowd. The big vase flashed in the sun like fire. There was a distant volley of drums. He gazed down at a trampled paper cap and poked it with his toe.

Mona said, "I wonder what they missed?"

"Missed?" Leland said. "Oh—you mean that woman with the vase. I don't know. A chance on another vase, maybe." He dropped his bottle under the bench. "How do you feel? I mean, there must be some place cooler than this."

"I'm all right," she said. "I feel fine."

"Well," he said. "I was just thinking." He smiled. "Were you serious about the Tunnel of Love?"

"I'm always serious," she said. "Especially about tunnels. Don't you know that by now?"

"I know everything," he said, and stood up. "I even know where it is. It's just around that corner—next to the

Dodge-Em. Or used to be."

It still was, and the rickety dock was deserted. Everybody had been drawn away to the pavilion. The woman at the ticket window was reading a magazine. She passed Leland his change without raising her head. An attendant with a toothpick in his mouth jerked a thumb at an empty boat, and yawned and turned his back. Mona chose a seat in the stern. Leland slid down beside her, and propped his heels on a thwart. The boat gave a quiver. It drifted slowly off on its hidden conveyor toward a grotto in a plaster mountain. There was a smell of damp and rotting wood. A newspaper floated by and vanished with the last of the light. The boat grated over a subterranean snag, nudged something metallic, and wallowed around a bend. Mona felt blindly down his arm for his hand.

"Oh, Lee," she said. "This is—"

"Yes," he said.

She moved in the dark. Her hand slipped up his arm again. "Lee," she said. "I can't even—"

"I can," he said.

He found her face with his mouth.

"I know," she said. "Oh, Lee. Oh, my darling."

The boat gave an exhausted lurch. There was a sunken grinding of chains. They swung heavily around another bend. The blackness dimmed to dark. In the distance, a shadow of light reached over the water. It broadened and brightened into day.

A voice said, "No."

Somebody laughed. The sound blew down the cavern with the sharpening light. It passed them like something tangible, bouncing from wall to wall.

"Uh, no," the voice said again. "I'm only—looking. I was just looking around."

Leland sat up with a jerk. He knew that voice. He had heard that startled, stammering voice before.

Mona released his arm. "It isn't over?" she said. "It isn't over already?"

"Wait," he said, and remembered. It was the voice on

the telephone. It was the voice of the stammering crank he had hung up on three weeks ago. He strained his eyes at the shimmering glare of the dock.

"Let's go again," Mona said. "I don't like all these people. I want to—"

"Yes," he said. "Sure—I'll get the tickets. I'll be right—"

He bounded onto the quaking planks. There were five men on the dock and three women. One of the men was the attendant. Near him stood a tall man in a sun helmet. Two of the others were soldiers with their hands in their pockets and their eyes on the women. The other was a short man with thick glasses and a Homburg hat on his head. Leland hesitated. The man in the sun helmet gave him a curious glance.

Leland went over to him.

"Excuse me," he said. "I wonder if you could tell me what time it is?"

The man looked him up and down and nodded. He reached in his trouser pocket and brought out what could have been a compact. He nodded again and pressed a hidden spring. A lid snapped open. He stared at the dial and snapped the lid back into place. Leland held his breath. The man smiled.

"Is four," he said. "Almost. A minute only is lacking."

"Thank you," Leland said. "Thanks very—"

He turned away. Mona smiled at him from the stern of their boat. The soldiers and two of the women were clambering into another. The man in the Homburg was gone.

SIX

Mona closed the door. She stood for a moment with her hand on the knob and tried to hold off desolation. But Sunday had ended with the click of the lock. It was all over again, and ended as it had never ended before. She listened to him going distantly down the hall. She heard the front door open and close. She thought she could hear the sound of his feet on the outside walk. The apartment was in the rear of the building. She couldn't even go to the window and see him on the sidewalk and keep him with her until he drove away. He was really gone now, and there was nothing left of Sunday. He had taken everything with him. It was only a little past nine. Monday didn't begin until tomorrow. Her fingers fell away from the knob. It might have been his unresponsive hand.

She turned from the door. It was just the door now. She was home again as she had been a thousand times before. The last ten days might never have happened. It might almost have been Ritchie who had gone away down the hall. The room closed in around her. It was like coming back to failure. This was what home had always been until the meeting by the street light on the corner. She faced the familiar smell, the familiar lamp that shaped the usual shadows among the familiar furniture, the familiar sense of something lost or lacking. She couldn't understand what had happened. There was no way of knowing even when it had happened or where. They had never been closer than on that first voyage through the Tunnel of Love, or farther apart than on the second. But the Big Dipper had flung them together again, and dinner in the secluded booth at the Savoy Grill had mended the break. He had even kissed her across the table when the waiter turned his back. And then— She walked to the sofa and sat miserably down, remembering the long silence during the long drive home, the indifferent kiss in the parked car, the abrupt parting in the hall.

There was so much she didn't understand. She wondered if she ever would. Experience seemed to teach her nothing. She looked back through their other days and nights. This wasn't the first time. It had happened before. His bottomless silence had forced them apart before tonight, and sat between them like a quarrel. It had risen between them during a long, rambling drive along the river, and then suddenly vanished over coffee at a truck-stop lunchroom on the highway. Only the night before last, when he had waited for her in the beer garden, it had driven her away the first time she had slipped out to talk for a moment. But an hour later he had pulled her to him and crushed her breathless with his heart pounding against her breast. This was the first time that the deep, antagonistic silence had followed them to the door. But there had been other times. There had been this afternoon. Her mind pounced on reassurance. There was still tomorrow night. He had said so. She remembered the words thrown at her at the door. It was all the proof she needed. Nothing could deny the need that was in them both. She opened her pocketbook and felt for a cigarette. Certainty had only faltered. Her hat slid off her lap to the floor, dropped and forgotten like doubt.

Tomorrow night, she promised herself. She lighted her cigarette, and became aware of the heat. She hadn't felt it until now. The restaurant had been air-conditioned. On the way home, anxiety had blunted every other sense. But she almost welcomed it. It brought back the park and this afternoon. She unbuttoned the top button on her dress, and saw her father coming through the twilight of the dining-room.

"Well, look who's here," he said.

Mona said, "Hello, Papa."

"I didn't hear you come in," he said. He explained everything with a smile. "I've been fixing myself a bite to eat." He had a sandwich in his hand and mayonnaise on his chin.

"I only came in a minute ago," she said.

The smile and the grinding jaws measured out the tedium and the distance to tomorrow night.

"Is that right," he said. "Did you have a nice time?"

"Very nice," she said. "We went out to Fairyland Park. And then we had dinner down at the Savoy." She looked away from the glint of interest in his eyes. She wouldn't share Leland with her father's appetite.

"The Savoy, eh," he said. "Well, what do you know about that." He nodded with satisfaction. It might have been he who had dined there. "The old Savoy."

"Yes," Mona said.

He wiped his mouth with the back of his hand, and took another bite. "I'll bet you had something good," he said. The sweat started on his face like envy. "But it's almost too hot to eat. I've just been picking all day."

"It's awful in here," Mona said.

"The climate is changing," her father said. He pushed the last of the sandwich into his mouth. His jaws ground up and down. "It never used to be like this. I never felt the heat like I have today."

Mona said, "I think I'll take a cold bath and go to bed."

Her father licked a spot of mayonnaise from his lip.

"The Savoy's an expensive place," he said. "He must be pretty well fixed." He began to fan himself with a folded newspaper. "I don't believe I caught his name. Did you tell me?"

"Oh," Mona said. She was surprised. "I thought you knew. I thought you all had introduced yourselves. His name is Sessions." She hesitated. "Leland Sessions." It was the first time she had said his name. Ritchie had asked her on that Friday night after the Sunflower, and twice since then, but she hadn't told him. She didn't know why. *But why should I?* she thought, and remembered the jealous color rising in the sallow face and the patch of mustache bristling. "I call him Lee," she said.

"Lee," her father said. "I don't suppose he's any kin to the overall people?" He smiled and fanned himself. "But he seemed like a fine young man. We had a nice talk."

"Yes," Mona said.

"To tell the truth," he said, "he made a fine impression on me. I liked his looks." He beat gently at the heat with the folded paper. "That was a fine Panama hat he had. He must have a good job. You could tell it was a genuine Panama."

"I guess so," Mona said.

"They weave them under water," he said. "But a good one lasts a lifetime. What kind of work does he do?"

"He used to work in some bank downtown," she said. "I don't know. I think it was the Cattlemen's Bank."

"Is that right," he said. "Well, that's—" The fan stopped moving. "Used to? You mean, he lost his job? They fired him?"

"No," Mona said. She stood up impatiently. She wanted Leland for herself. "He's on a leave of absence or something. Whatever they call it."

"Oh," he said. He resumed his smile and his fanning. "Oh—I see. Well, that's different."

Mona said, "I think I'll go to bed, Papa." She stooped for her hat and pocketbook, and felt a kind of guilt. It couldn't be much past nine-thirty. "It's so hot," she said, offering the only reason she could find.

But her father held her with his endless unsatisfied smile. The Panama hat and the expensive dinner and the Buick coupé had not yet been fully explained.

"His family has some money," she said, and tried to pretend that this wasn't Lee she was justifying to her father. "I don't think he has to work. He only does it because he likes to."

"Is that a fact," he said. "Well, what do you know about that." He shook his head and stared. "He's a lucky boy." He sank into a chair. "Come to think of it, there used to be a family by that name up in St. Joseph. They were pretty well fixed. I wonder if he's any kin to—"

"I don't know," Mona said, and brushed a kiss on the top of his head. "Good night, Papa. I think you'd better go to bed, too. You'll be more comfortable with your clothes off."

"Yes, indeed," he said, and reached for the remains of the Sunday paper. "You run right along. Good night."

Mona turned away, and began to unbutton her dress. Behind her, as she went down the hall to her room, she could hear him rustling the pages of the sports section. He had read it all this morning: the predictions, the statistics, the solemn discussions of strategy. But he had forgotten it all by now. They had slipped from his mind like Leland's face and name. It would all be as good as new.

Mona turned on the light and closed the door, and stepped out of her dress. Her body faced her in the dressing-table mirror. She watched her breasts emerge from the brassière. She would have given anything if the hands on the clasp were Leland's. But memory was enough. She kicked off her shoes, and raced toward the moment when the night would close around her and she could remember the darkness of the Tunnel of Love. She wanted to think of all that her strength and love had done, and all there was yet to do. The thought of him ran through her like pain. There was nothing else in the world, and nothing had ended but Sunday.

SEVEN

The moon was up, small and white and faraway. It spread a film of frost over the rooftops. Under the heavy trees on Brush Creek Boulevard the moonlight lay like scattered leaves. The heat hung on, crouching in the closed places, defying the night. Leland drove slowly along with the rest of the tired and sweltering traffic. Sunday had ended. There was no place to go but home.

His gloom touched everything with unreality: the strolling couples under the blanketing trees, the bridge games on the screened porches, the panting cars at the gaudy drive-in places. He was alone. He was removed from it all. It was what he had thought he needed. But now he couldn't be sure. The dark familiar depression was wheeling back again. He watched the unrealities sweep by, and the depression clotted his mind like fatigue. The Panama hat lay beside him on the seat, where Mona had left it. It was like a distant glimpse of happiness. At the traffic light he pulled up with all the other cars, and waited in a vacuum among the scraps of the surrounding conversations and the murmurs of muted radios. He gazed at the hat on the seat, and thought again of the man in the Homburg. But it wasn't that. He would have liked to be sure that his had been the voice on the telephone, but it didn't really matter. It wasn't his curiosity that was unsatisfied. He wondered what it was that really mattered. The only certainty was that it wasn't this. It couldn't be this empty journey toward the inevitable moment with his mother in the hall or in the living-room or on the stairs. It wasn't the inevitable ambush of memory behind the bedroom door.

The signal changed. A car in the next lane leaped growling forward and a horn blared from a car behind. The Plaza glittered out below, all lights and tile and tinted stucco. He swung across the intersection, and into Forty-Seventh Street. The car jarred over a cavity in the pavement and the hat bounced gently on the seat. He reached over and pushed it safely back from the edge. It was his only real link with the afternoon and happiness and suffiency. He wanted to believe that tomorrow night he would again be glad to see her. But his mind went limp. It was like trying to experience another person's pleasure. A dark car went by and a white face stared.

Leland stared glumly back. He couldn't even summon up contempt. Something was lacking. Between the Tunnel of Love and the Savoy Grill and the apartment on Charlotte Street, he had lost something, and he didn't know what it was.

At the foot of the hill a gasoline station sat in a bleak oasis of colored light: an expanse of concrete, a whitewashed brick office, and an avenue of pumps. It wasn't the station he usually patronized, but it was the only one in sight still open. He rolled up the slope of the driveway and stopped at a yellow pump. He could see the attendant sitting at a desk in the little office. He had a cigar in his mouth and his eyes were fixed on nothing. Leland waited, leaning over the wheel. He was in no hurry. He was only going home. A truck rumbled down the hill, with a ground chain jumping and clanging. He lighted a cigarette, and the attendant moved his head and saw him. Leland watched him put down the cigar and hop to his feet and trot briskly out. He was a stocky man in white coveralls, with a wispy blond mustache. He trotted up to the car, assembling a jaunty smile.

"Yes, sir," he said. "What can I do you for?"

"Fill it up," Leland said. "It ought to take about ten, I think."

"Okey doke," the attendant said.

He walked to the pump and reached for the hose, and stopped. A look of indecision wavered across his face. He peered back at the car, thoughtfully biting his lip. The pale mustache twitched like a nerve. He took his hand from the hose.

"Say," he said. He walked slowly back to the car. His shoulders swayed elaborately, like a wrestler's. He halted at the door, and nodded. "Wait just a minute," he said.

"Yes?" Leland said. He glanced at the pump. "Can't you reach it?"

"I knew I'd seen you somewheres," the attendant said.

Leland stared at him.

"Yeah." the attendant said. "I thought I recognized you."

"Recognized me?" Leland said. For an instant he really didn't understand. He had sunk below distrust.

The attendant spat between his feet, and gave the car an ugly look. His lips drew back against his teeth. He thrust his face close to the window.

"You thought I'd wait on you?" he said. "By God, you are a crusty bastard. I wouldn't wait on you if— Get out of here. Beat it."

He made a sudden gesture with a grimy hand. It had the force of a revelation. So this was how they felt. It was as though Mona had betrayed him into trust. But now he knew. Nothing had changed. Reality was this thrusting face, this hand on the door handle. They had stared and whispered and laughed, and he had made himself believe that it meant no more than that. But now— He looked at hatred, and violence. The pretense had ended. It was in the open now.

The attendant jerked his head.

"Get going," he said. "You and your goddamned Buick both. This is still a free country. There's no law says I've got to sell gas to every—"

Leland let his hands slip off the wheel. Here was what they had really felt all these months. Here was what had been hidden behind the glances and the whispers and the jeering laughter. He threw his cigarette out the opposite window, and the weight of depression sloughed away. The enemy had declared himself, and it was what he had been waiting for.

The attendant let go of the door handle and stepped back.

"Beat it," he said. "You heard me—get going."

Leland reached for the door.

He said, "What did you call me?"

The attendant had turned away. He stopped and looked back, with astonishment.

He said, "Are you trying to start something?"

It was the final goad to anger. Leland pushed the door open with his foot. They didn't expect resistance. They thought they had broken him to his corner. He slid from under the wheel.

The attendant said, "Now, look out there—"

Leland took a step toward him. He hadn't been in a fight for years, but rage was enough. It gave him strength. He didn't need skill and experience.

"You called me a bastard." he said. "Wasn't that it?"

"I told you to get out of here," he attendant said. He stared at Leland with amazement, as though he couldn't believe his eyes. "I said—"

"I know what you said," Leland said.

"Look out, now," the attendant said. His mouth was twisted. His mustache seemed to have slipped askew. "I'm warning you—"

It could almost have been an accident. Leland didn't even know he had moved until he felt the wrench of pain in his hand, and saw the attendant stumbling back against the edge of the concrete island. He stood like a spectator, watching the man shake his head. Incredibly, his anger was gone. It had spent itself in one unremembered blow.

"Okay," the attendant said. "Okay, you bastard."

The short, excited jab caught Leland on the cheek. It was a light, awkward thump. He scarcely felt it. But it brought terror swooping down upon him: the big detective in the cowboy belt advanced again across the bare official room, slapping the rolled magazine against his leg. Leland stood as he had stood before the locked door. The attendant struck him again, a hard, solid blow on the ear. It might have been the rolled magazine smashing down on his head. He ducked away, as he had ducked the other time.

"Okay," the attendant said. "Now, maybe—"

The sound of his voice brought Leland back. This wasn't authority. The police had released him. This was only the enemy. The dying anger revived. He struck out and missed. Something struck him a shattering blow in the chest. His breath went out in a gasp. He threw up his hands before his face and tried to retreat. He bumped into a pump. The attendant was after him like a cat. Pain burst through his chin. He tripped over something and went down.

"I wish she could see you now," the attendant said. "I wish to God she could—"

Leland sat dazed on the driveway in a smear of oil. A bare knee poked like a broken bone through a tear in his trousers. He looked dully up. The attendant stood over him.

"Get up, you," the man said. He was breathing hard and his mustache was stained with blood. "I'm not through with you yet."

The attendant hit him twice before he reached his feet. Leland reeled away. Something kept him from falling and something cleared his head. He felt his fist hit something hard.

The attendant said, "I'll—"

Leland dived at him. But rage wasn't enough. He fell against the car.

The attendant said, "I wish to God she could see you now."

Leland didn't know what he was talking about. His arms were too heavy to lift. The weight tipped him forward, and the attendant knocked him down. He sank like a man in deep water.

Leland slowly raised his head. He was squatting on the concrete island near the middle pump. The attendant stood a couple of yards away. One big hand was rubbing the knuckles of the other. He was watching him with a kind of embarrassment.

They regarded each other uneasily. The intimacy of anger was gone. They might have been strangers who had hailed each other by mistake. The attendant started to speak, and didn't. Instead, he took out a handkerchief and wiped his mouth and blew his nose.

Leland pushed his hair back and stood up. He stood for a moment, swaying. Something turned in his head, and tumbled and settled into balance. He limped across the pavement to his car. Pain stabbed at him from every direction. It made every step an agony. But he welcomed it. Pain was a block to thought. It gave him a moment of respite. For a while he could believe that he wasn't hated and hounded. He could believe that he was only hurt.

PART THREE

ONE

Winger ʼCROUCHED IN THE SHRUBBERY ACROSS the street from the Sessions house, and waited. At the moment, it was all he could do. He had lost them again, an hour ago, at a traffic signal on Wornall Road. His 1929 Essex was no match for a year-old Buick. But it wasn't speed that would count in the end. Persistence and guile were all he needed. During the past few weeks he had proved that often enough. He peered through the darkness at the darkened house to which the murderer would sooner or later return, and counted up his triumphs.

Guile alone had saved him last Sunday on the dock at the Tunnel of Love. The memory of that perilous moment quickened his heart with delight. But persistence had been even more rewarding. Sessions's haunts and habits were as familiar to him now as his own. Winger ticked them off in his mind: *Foley's,* the Sunflower, and the Savoy Grill, the 14th green at the Blue Hills Country Club and a dead-end lane on the road to Shawnee Mission, the apartment on Charlotte Street and a dozen nameless bars and beer parlors. He even knew the dark-haired waitress's name. An afternoon of patient inquiry had finally told him that.

But Winger refused to delude himself. He was willing to face the facts. The evidence was mounting, but it wasn't yet complete. There were still some unanswered questions.

The relationship of Sessions and the girl needed further clarification. Were they lovers as well as confederates? It might be useful to know. What was Mr. Foley's role? Winger fanned himself with his hat, and wondered. He was inclined to believe that the old man was only peripherally involved. The chances were that he was merely a tool. There was also the significance of the fight in the filling station. That had seemed at first to be a lead of major importance. He chose to doubt it now. His interview with the attendant the following evening had been brief but persuasive. Nothing of real value could be learned there.

Winger shifted his position. He didn't mind the discomfort of twining creepers and tickling leaves. That was part of the life of an investigator. But he had exhausted the possibilities of the dark house and the silent trees. The weeks of watching and following and listening had conditioned him to action. He felt for his flashlight pencil, trained the tiny beam on his watch, and started. It was twenty-five minutes to four. He had been here almost two hours. Where had they gone? What were they doing? In two hours almost anything could happen. They might even— The thought gave him a prick of panic. But it couldn't be. That would be too wild and ironic a coincidence. It wasn't possible that this could be the night of nights. He couldn't be defeated by an accident of speed.

But the possibility snapped his patience. He started to his feet and took a distracted step, and almost failed to hear the car in time. A reflex saved him. He collapsed in a sculpture of privet. The headlights swung harmlessly overhead. There was a crunch of tires on gravel. Winger raised his head. It was Sessions. A taillight blinked through the foliage across the street, and vanished. He adjusted his glasses and found his hat and stood cautiously up. But there was no real need for caution now. He had only to move quietly and stay in the shadows. The night was on his side again. He slipped around the privet and ducked behind a tree. It might even be possible to cross the street.

There was a clump of cedars not far from the door. They would give him shelter and a close-range view when Sessions came around from the rear. There was no telling what a good look at that face might reveal.

This time he didn't hear the car at all. He was only aware of a sudden burst of light. With his hat in his hand, he stopped and stared blindly back.

A voice said, "All right, Mac. Just stand where you are."

Winger stood.

"And keep those hands away from your pocket," the voice said.

A car door opened and a heel ground on the sidewalk. Something poked him hard in the back. He took an involuntary step.

"That's right," the voice said. "Over to the car."

The light dimmed, or shifted. Vision slowly returned. A dark car emerged from the glare. Winger made out the eye of a spotlight and a door hanging open. A hand slapped him twice on the buttocks, and felt under his shoulders and across his chest. The pressure withdrew from his back. He turned his head and looked at a khaki shirt and a silver badge and a dark hand holding a revolver. Reason returned like vision. There was no cause for alarm. It was only the police.

A voice from the car said, "Okay, Tony? Need any help?"

The other policeman laughed. "Not unless he falls down," he said. He turned to Winger. His voice hardened. "Out pretty late, aren't you, Mac? What's the story? Been peeping?"

Winger swallowed.

"Uh," he said. "No, I—" He tried to think. "I'm afraid you've made a—mistake."

"Yeah?" the policeman said. "About what?"

"About what I'm doing," Winger said. "I'm not a— My name is Winger. I work for the *Star*. I'm a reporter."

The man in the car gave a grunt. "Now I've heard everything," he said.

"Okay," the other policeman said. "Let's see it—the press card, Mac. Or did you forget and leave it at home?"

"No," Winger said. "I mean, yes. I've got it right—" He drew out his wallet and folded it open and handed it over. "I'm on an assignment."

The policeman didn't reply. He took the wallet and walked over to the car and held the card in the light.

"Francis K. Winger," he said. "Lives at 3319 Tracy. Blue eyes. Brown hair. Five foot five. Weighs one-fifty. It looks okay." He returned the wallet. "What's the K stand for?"

"Uh," Winger said. "I— That's my middle name. It's Kennebec."

"Okay, Kennebec," the policeman said. "So you're a reporter. So you're on an assignment. Like what?"

Winger hesitated. But there was no alternative to the truth. He said, "I'm watching—well, that house over there. It's a special investigation. That's the Sessions home. It's where Louise Heim was murdered It's in connection with that."

The policeman stared at him.

"Oh, for God's sake," the man in the car said. "I—" He gave a kind of laugh.

The other policeman said, "Well—what do you think?"

"I don't," the man in the car said. "I stopped trying to figure out the *Star* a long time ago."

"It sounds nutty enough," the other policeman said.

"It's nutty enough for me," the man in the car said. "Kiss Kennebec good night, and let's go."

"Okay," the other policeman said. He gave Winger a clap on the back. "Stay in there, Kennebec. Only next time, keep your hands out of your pockets. That's the . . ."

Winger didn't hear the rest of it. Something had moved in the shadows of the cedar clump across the street. It could only be Sessions on his way to the door. The police had bungled the case again. They had made him miss his chance.

TWO

A GRAY SUN SANK IN A BLACK-AND-WHITE SKY, a tear ran down a monstrous smiling face, and a hundred unseen violins sobbed and shrilled and soared sadly into silence. The giant curtains trembled and closed on the last restrained embrace. Love had triumphed once again over every conceivable obstacle. The lights came on like magic. From the enormous dome of the ceiling a multitude of tiny stars twinkled down on all the sham luxury: the useless columns, the winged cupids, the plaster nudes, the lavish tarnished gold. Everybody squirmed and muttered and looked about.

Leland sat expectantly for a moment with all the rest. But he had lost interest. He was beyond the reach of any catharsis now. The film had failed him like the books and the magazines and the newspapers. He couldn't abandon reality. The rest of the program would be only two more hours of waiting. He stood up and worked past the implacable knees, and into the plodding crowd in the aisle. Another unseen orchestra struck up a waltz. The curtains stirred again and the lights faded out. There was a ripple of applause from somewhere in the balcony. He inched stiffly along to the foyer. Sitting had tightened his injured leg again.

Three small boys broke around him as he went down the padded steps to the smoking-room. There was a smell of tobacco and sweat and disinfectant. He took his place with the others at the long mirror. Beside him, an usher in an anachronistic uniform gloomily inspected a moraine of blemishes on his forehead. Farther along, somebody buried his face in the sink and blew like a whale, and a small man in thick glasses tugged gravely at his necktie. The three small boys emerged loudly from one of the toilets. A man with aggressive shoulders and a furtive chin loitered near the urinals, smoking a cigarette and glancing at everybody with an air of tentative friendliness.

Leland felt the usual stir of recognition start and quicken. It didn't matter. *Let them look,* he thought. *Let them stare their heads off.* He had nothing to fear from any of them in here. There were too many of them to constitute a threat. The filling-station attendant last Sunday night had shown him where to look for danger. His safety lay in numbers. Danger was the man encountered alone, or the ready and waiting group. But this was just a crowd of strangers. Suspicion was all that any of them had in common yet. He moved away before they could unite in purpose, and went quickly up the stairs and through the protection of the new crowd in the lobby and on to the larger crowd on the sidewalk. The clutch of heat in the street took his breath away. The neon signs were as red as fire and every light blazed like a flame. A long, wilted queue stretched from the box office almost to the corner. The empty faces gave him an empty glance. A blind man crept by with a cardboard sign on his chest and his dead eyes fixed on the dead windows of the office buildings across the street. In a shop window, five mannikins in fur coats stood in complicated attitudes around a placard in an ornate frame: *20% Off.*

Leland walked slowly through the draining heat. He had no destination except the parking lot where he had left his car. Mona was the only alternative to home. But it was still too early for that. She wouldn't be free for another hour or two. Halfway up the block he turned at random into a cigar store. A clerk rose up from behind the counter with a box of cigars in each hand and pencil between his teeth. Leland bought a package of cigarettes, and went out and on. There was a bar next door to the cigar store. He didn't really want a drink, but the heat made up his mind. The door fell open at a touch. It might have been a trap. A blast of cold, stale air chilled the sweat on his face. He slumped at the bar and ordered a drink, and wearily looked around at what had now become the background of his life. There was the usual throbbing juke box, the usual smell of beer, the usual fuddled stares. He took a sip of his watery drink, and thought again of Mona. She was more than an alternative. She alone disguised the sameness and the change.

The bartender opened a bottle of Coca Cola and dropped a cube of ice into a glass. He was sullen and sallow and overweight. Leland watched him walk down the bar with the glass and the bottle. He slid them in front of a small man in a dark suit and thick glasses. The man turned his head. Behind the heavy lenses his pale eyes slowly and heavily blinked. Leland caught his breath. He knew that face. He had seen it no more than ten minutes ago, in the men's room at the theater. It was the man who had stood just down the mirror and tightened the knot of his necktie. He lowered his head and picked up his drink, and told himself that the man's presence here meant nothing. There were probably a dozen others in the place who had also come from the theater. But the man had already seen him twice. It might be well not to tempt providence too far. He motioned to the bartender and paid for his drink. There were other bars on Twelfth Street.

The next bar was three doors away. He went in—to the same small room, the same damp coolness, the same sad and sodden crowd. There was a small piano instead of a juke box. A woman in an extravagant gown struck a chord, and began to sing:

"Come on over to my house, baby,
Nobody home but me . . ."

Leland found a place at the bar between a cabdriver and two bald and blue-jowled salesmen. They gave him a sightless glance, and one of the salesmen moved a grudging inch.

The other one said, "I run into Bloom up at Omaha."

"Bloom?" the first one said. "Arnold Bloom?"

"Morris," the other one said. "With Playtime Frocks. He had his new wife with him."

The first one grunted, and said nothing. They lifted their glasses. The cabdriver tipped a few grains of salt into a glass of beer, took a swallow, and reached for the shaker again. At a table in a corner, a man with a Band-Aid saddling his nose raised a jigger of whisky, and smiled to himself. He tossed it off at a gulp, like medicine or hope. Leland tried to catch the bartender's eye. But he had turned his back to mix a complicated drink.

The door opened. Leland turned his head with the others. The small man with the thick glasses came hesitantly in. His winter suit was baggy with heat and he had a felt hat under his arm. Their eyes didn't meet. Leland ducked his head behind the cabdriver's shoulders. He crouched with his eyes on the swimming bar, too stricken to think. The woman at the piano sang:

> *"Ain't nobody, baby,*
> *Home but me . . ."*

One of the salesmen said, "The big trouble with Bloom . . ."

Leland told himself that it couldn't be a coincidence. It couldn't be by accident that the man who had stood beside him in the washroom and who had watched him in the other bar had now followed him here. It couldn't be an accident this time. But there was no use trying to hide. The man could hardly have failed to see him by now. He lifted his head. In the back-bar mirror he saw the heavy face and the heavy glasses framed between a man in a pale-gray Stetson and a woman with pale-blue hair.

The bartender trudged across the reflection.

"Yes, sir," he said. "What was yours?"

Leland said, "I—" The thick glasses glinted again in the mirror. "Never mind," he said, and slid off the stool. "I just remembered something."

Instinct carried him through the door, and left him stranded on the sidewalk. Somebody stepped abruptly aside and gave him an understanding smile. He tried to think. But there was nothing to guide him now. This was a new attack. He wasn't prepared for a return to indirection. The fight in the filling station had adjusted him to action. He thought: *He's following me.* There was no other explanation. *But why? He could have spoken to me in the washroom. What does he want? Who is he? When did—* Confusion pulled his mind limp. Across the street a hawker was selling sheet music in a loud and whining voice. Leland wandered a few blundering steps up the sidewalk behind two chattering couples, past a shoe-shining parlor, and stopped.

Something made him turn. The small man was standing at the entrance to the bar in a pink flush of neon. His hat was no longer under his arm. It was fixed squarely on his head, and it was no longer just a hat. It was a Homburg. Leland stood rooted. The last hopeful doubt gave way. He knew now why he had known that face. He wasn't only the man in the washroom. He was also the man on the dock, and the threatening voice on the telephone. The man sidled away from the door. He glanced once up the street, and instantly became absorbed in a display of nylon stockings. Leland tried to move. His memory gave another lurch. It showed him a prowl car throbbing at the curb and two men conferring in the beam of a spotlight. One of them was a policeman in uniform. The other wore glasses and a dark-blue suit. He hadn't known what to make of it at the time. He had supposed that the little man was one of the neighborhood watchmen. The depth of his credulity staggered him, like a blow. His mind caved in.

Fright made the decision for him. He was plunging up

the street at almost a run before he realized what he was doing. But he pulled himself up in time. He couldn't lose his head now. Running wouldn't help. It would only arouse the other enemy, and bring them all down upon him. He told himself that his one chance lay in inconspicuous haste. The crowd was thicker at the corner. He twisted unobtrusively through. He had a start of almost half a block. In spite of everything, hope circled slowly back. He surged with the others across the street. But he needed more than half a block. The little detective hadn't been outdistanced yet. He could feel him there, in the crowd at his back, pressing easily along, trained and experienced in relentlessness.

He stumbled over a curbing. In front of the Hotel Muehlebach a porter with an armload of luggage blocked his way. He tried to shove his way past.

Somebody said, "What's your hurry?"

The abrupt voice tripped his stride. He collided with a group of men shaking hands. Somebody caught his arm.

"Hey—"

A suitcase knocked against his knee. The hand gripped his shoulder. It was all over. He turned around.

Preston Smith, in a white dinner jacket, shook his arm, and grinned.

"Lee," he said. His face was sunburned and his eyes were faintly bloodshot. "How in the hell are you?"

Only the hand on his arm kept him from falling. The past smiled at him, and he hardly recognized it.

"Long time no see," Preston said. "Where in the hell have you been all summer? Come on down to the Grill. We're just . . ."

The crowd swarmed around them. Somewhere among the shifting faces the slow, deliberate eyes of the detective were peering through the thick lenses, searching him out. Duplicity began to lead him toward the hotel entrance. Treachery murmured cheerfully in his ear.

Leland said, "Let go of me."

With a jerk he tore his arm free, and threw himself

away. Reason fell behind. The sweat of panic streamed down his face. He thought he heard someone call out as he lunged across the street, but he didn't listen. Ahead of him lay the dark mouth of an alley. Darkness was shelter and safety. He was running now, past caring who saw him or who stared at him or who wondered. They were closing in on him. He didn't know why. But he knew that they would never get him.

Leland lay like a sack in the doorway, and gulped for breath. His heart knocked like a fist and there was a burning pain in his side. His collar strangled him, but he hadn't the strength to get it loose. He had no idea where he was. Panic had chosen the way and exhaustion had picked the place. He sat up in a mess of windblown paper and broken glass, and waited for strength to come back.

Time drifted by. It could have been hours or minutes. From the doorway he had a view of an empty cobbled street and a row of dark warehouses beyond. A mailbox stood like a sentinel under a street light at the corner. There was no sound but a distant grumble that might have been a streetcar, and the anonymous whispers of the night. He began to feel a kind of convalescent calm. His will came back with his wind. He couldn't stay here. He got heavily to his feet. There would be a street sign at the corner under the light. He trudged through the warm, dead silence. His steps made the only sound. He came out on Nineteenth Street. The lights of Main Street and familiarity beckoned from a block away. He wondered if it would be safe to take a streetcar back to the parking lot and his car. A picture of home rose up in his mind, like a promise of rest and sanctuary. It was all that drew him on.

The warning touched him before he reached the corner. He couldn't go back to the parking lot. The detective would be there. He had probably been there for an hour or more, safely concealed and waiting. The little strength that had begun to revive suddenly seeped away. Exhaustion saved him from despair. It left him beyond caring. He drove himself on to Main Street, but he didn't stop. Instead, he turned to the left, away from his car, away from rest, away from danger. There was no fight left in him. He had burned it up in panic and in flight. But somewhere he might be able to find a place to hide.

A streetcar went by in a blaze of light and purpose. It was going his way, but it was gone before he happened to think. He passed a bar and a huddle of rooms-by-the-hour hotels, and mounted the ramp of the viaduct that bridged the railroad yards. A dozen taxicabs dozed at the curb in front of the Union Station. Every nodding driver might have been an agent of the police, ready to seize and hold him. With the last of his strength, he dodged among the sheltering cars in the parking area. The flaming crown of the Liberty Memorial shaft blackened the sky on the hill ahead. He climbed the endless shallow steps toward the soaring blaze. It told him his destination.

Beyond the Memorial Building, the mannered rusticity of the park sloped darkly and distantly away in groves and lawns and scenic drives. He wasn't alone. He could hear the stifled giggles behind the bushes, the encouraging protests under the trees, and the sighs and the snores of the sleepers. They surrounded him with safety. Privacy was respected here. He let himself down in the lee of a glacial rock. There might be better places farther on, but this was as far as he could go. He loosened his necktie and unbuttoned his collar and stared up at the limitless sky, trying to see ahead to tomorrow. But tonight gripped his mind. All he could see was the detective following him through the night. His innocence had persuaded no one, not even the police. The meaningless weeks dissolved like hope. He was back in June again.

THREE

LELAND EMERGED FROM THE PARK in the first blue light of morning. His throat was dry and his clothes were damp and he itched and ached all over. In the west, above the smokeless stacks of industry, the last stars flickered out. He remembered the other dawn outside the roadhouse in the County with Mona, and the illusion of a calm, new, friendly world. Well, he was less ingenuous now. He supposed that there had been somebody watching him even then.

The same cabs waited at the curb in front of the Union Station. He could hear a train chuffing in the yards below, and a slow bell ringing. A dog sauntered around the equestrian statue in the dusty green island of Washington Square. The shades were drawn in the saloon on the corner. In the narrow lobby of the Plaza Hotel a woman with a goiter slashed at the floor with a mop. There was an all-night diner next door. He wasn't hungry. He wasn't anything. Four hours of sleep had left him only awake. But it was time for breakfast. He opened the door and went in.

Three men in overalls sat slumped at the counter. They turned and stared and slumped back down again. Work had loosened their mouths and dulled their eyes, and shaped a likeness that could have been a family resemblance. It was impossible to guess whether they were beginning or ending a day. Leland took a stool near the door and gazed at a counter display of rolls. Overhead a ceiling fan sluggishly stirred the air. The counterman came up the aisle with his eyes on the clock. It was twenty minutes after five. He said nothing. He only looked and waited, as though he had been granted arrogance as a compensation for long hours and inadequate pay.

"A cup of coffee," Leland said. "And a couple of those doughnuts."

The counterman grunted. He opened the case and reached for a plate.

"You want cream in that coffee?" he said. "Or black?"

"Black," Leland said.

The counterman turned his back. A handkerchief stained with lipstick trailed from his hip pocket like a tail. The three men in overalls rose together and filed out. A boy came in with a bundle of newspapers under his arm. The counterman slid a mug of coffee up the counter. He turned his back again and began to comb his hair. Leland took a sip of coffee. It tasted faintly of oil. The doughnuts stuck to his teeth like paper. Only idleness made him eat. He stared at himself in the mirroring flank of the coffee urn, and hardly knew his grimy, sweat-streaked face. A kind of anger hardened his jaw. He was Leland Sessions, but this was where he had to come for breakfast. He had been driven to hide in a doorway and to sleep in his clothes in a park. He stirred his oily coffee. The enemy was grinding him down like poverty.

A dog-eared *Star,* folded open to the crossword puzzle, lay abandoned on a nearby stool. It was yesterday's Late Sports Final, but Leland picked it up. Anything was better than thinking. But someone had solved the puzzle, and sealed it with a lumpy smear of what looked like chile con carne. He turned a ragged page: "Rockslide Mars Ozark Shrine." His gaze dropped blindly down the paragraphs. It wandered on to "Joplin Man a Blaze Victim," and away. A smiling girl in an evening dress waved from the top of the page: "4-H Queen To Wed Stunt Flier." Beyond her stretched a waste of radio listings. There was no distraction there. He drifted back to the Joplin man: "Cincinnati, August 26 (AP).—The toll of a flash fire that early yesterday destroyed the Little Reno Club here rose to seven with the death at City Hospital today of Rex Corn, 31, of Joplin, Mo. Corn, who died without regaining consciousness, was identified by fingerprints after police . . ." He pushed the paper away. But the word had already pierced the fragile film of anesthesia. Reality was back.

"Anything else?"

It was the counterman.

"No, thanks," Leland said. He dropped a quarter on the counter and stood up. "I don't suppose you've got a washroom in here?"

The counterman swept the mug and plate under the counter.

"All the way back," he said. "And don't forget to flush it."

"Thanks," Leland said. "I'll try."

When he came out on the street again, it was full morning. The air was already dead with heat. A streetcar passed with a row of glum faces. He crossed to the shabby triangle of grass, and sat down on a bench. The name of the city was stenciled on its back like an assumption of guilt and its legs were set securely in a concrete base. A factory whistle began to whine. He tried to order his thoughts. For the moment, he was safe. No one had followed him here. He also had all he needed to know. He knew now who the enemy was, and what they wanted. Deception explained everything. He lighted a cigarette and thought of that last afternoon at Police Headquarters: the friendly smiles, the hearty handshakes, and the Chief of Detectives saying, "We certainly have appreciated your co-operation, Mr. Sessions." Even the big detective had pumped his hand and grinned. He supposed the man in the Homburg hat and the thick glasses had already been given his orders. But he could match their cunning. He was calm and cool and ready. This wasn't last night. He was done with panic.

Leland sat on the bench with the oily coffee still bitter in his mouth, and told himself that the evidence could hardly be plainer. The proof of prearrangement was everywhere he looked. There had been no withdrawal of suspicion in the newspapers. They had reported his last interrogation, and after that, nothing. The case had dropped from the news. It was obvious that the police had hoped to disarm him with silence. They were waiting for him to betray himself. Then they would rise and strike. The knowledge jerked him to his feet and into motion. But he held himself down to a walk. It would do no good to run now. Danger patrolled the city. He could see the whole devious plan at last. He couldn't protect himself from betrayal. His innocence didn't matter any more. They only wanted a reasonable facsimile of proof. Their aim was simply a conviction. They no longer cared who really murdered Louise Heim. They only wanted a victim. They only wanted him. A one-armed man shuffled up the path in an explosion of pigeons, dragging a bag of refuse, spearing yesterday's litter. Leland dropped his cigarette and licked his lips. He could feel the net drawing closer around him.

A lump of fear crept up his throat. But he held it back. He couldn't lose his head again. There was no way of knowing what they could twist into evidence. An indictment would be the beginning of the end. The enemy would sit in the jury box. His only hope was to disappear. Once out of their reach, he would be safe. They couldn't yet have assembled all the proofs that were needed. They were still committed to watching and waiting. Well, let them wait. Let them watch. Let them try to trap him into guilt. He knew where safety lay. It was anywhere but here. He should have known that weeks ago. But the enemy had hounded him too hard. The endless skirmishes had faltered reason. Flight was his last best weapon, and the time had come to use it.

Leland quickened his pace. He had an objective now. The first step was to get his car. There was no alternative to that. He had to have it. They could watch him if they wished. They could follow him home. Then he would prepare his departure. There was nothing they could do to stop him. The smiles and the handshakes and the genial farewells were permission to do as he pleased. He had no regrets. The enemy had cut his roots here. Kansas City stood only for danger. There was nothing and nobody here to hold him any more. Even Mona— The haste and certainty dribbled out of his stride. Safety could be loneliness. Safety alone could be cold and remote. He told himself uneasily that it didn't matter. But the one forgotten tie dug into his mind like doubt. He remembered isolation. It was as though the enemy had tricked him into a fatal vacillation.

He joined an elderly man at the streetcar stop, and tried not to think of her warmth and her sympathy and her love. But the memory had cut too deeply. He couldn't shake it out. Just across the street, at the foot of the Main Street hill, a streetcar waited for the traffic signal to change. The old man gave him a faded, senile glance. Leland wondered where he would be tomorrow, and if it would be safe to write. But he didn't want a page of lifeless words. He didn't want to live with a piece of white paper and a scribbled name. He wanted her. They had taken everything else. He wanted her and he needed her. Safety wasn't enough.

The traffic lights blinked off, and on. The streetcar came swaying across the street. He had the feeling that time was running out. The old man stirred expectantly. Leland looked at loneliness, and knew he couldn't leave her behind. The streetcar ground to a stop. The doors sprang open. The old man moved with astonishing alacrity. But Leland was ahead of him. He thrust him aside with a kind of ferocious delight. He was breaking out, but he wasn't going alone. He was taking Mona with him. He was on his way, but it wasn't flight. It was an elopement.

FOUR

His voice was faint and hurried. Mona had the feeling that he was telephoning from another city.

She said, "Where are you?"

"What?" he said. The faint voice hesitated. "What do you mean? I'm home. But—"

"Oh," Mona said. "I didn't mean—" An impulse to giggle panicked her thoughts. "I just—I don't know."

It was all completely unreal. Even the familiar voice might have belonged to someone else. *But I knew,* she thought. *I was sure. I knew from the very beginning.* And it was his voice. Her fingers tightened with a kind of greed on the receiver, pressing it hard against her ear.

Leland said, "Hello?"

"Yes," she said. "Yes."

She could hear her father in the bathroom, splashing water in the basin. *Please,* she thought. *Please make him wait. Please don't have him come out now.*

"Well?" Leland said.

"Do you have to ask?" she said. "Don't you know? Oh, Lee—of course I will."

"No," he said. "But I—"

His voice was suddenly muffled. The line hummed and crackled and sang. All she could hear was a faraway murmur. It didn't matter. There was a whole lifetime ahead of them.

"Lee," she said. "Oh, Lee. I love you so much."

The noises in the line trailed off in a gentle hissing.

"What?" he said. "I'm sorry. It's this damn connection. But, anyway. Look—can you be ready in about thirty minutes?"

"I'm ready now," she said, standing naked beneath the pink flowered robe and with her dark hair still tangled from sleep. "I've always been—"

"Good," he said. "I'll— Somebody's coming. I can't talk any more."

His receiver slammed like a door. Mona put down the telephone and turned limply away. Thirty minutes was too long to wait, and too little time for all she had to do Urgency held her rooted. It was hard to believe that only five minutes ago she was only getting ready for work.

There was no sound now from the bathroom. She faced the warning silence. A door creaked sharply open. Her father rolled cheerfully up the passage, whistling a medley of juke-box tunes. His big face gleamed with happiness and lotion. He abandoned song for a smile. She could only think of what she couldn't say.

"I thought I heard the phone," he said.

Mona nodded.

"It was Lee," she said. "He wanted to ask me something."

"Oh?" he said.

"It was just about a date."

"Oh," he said.

His smile drifted aimlessly away. It alighted on the sideboard. He put out a hand and picked up a crumpled bag of potato chips.

"Empty," he said. "That's funny. I could have sworn—"

"You finished them last night," Mona said.

"So I did," he said. "But I thought I'd left a few." He crushed the bag and sighed. "Well, I guess I ought to get on over to the store." He hitched up his trousers. "You come along when—"

"Yes," she said, and changed her mind. There was a better way. "I'm sorry, Papa. I meant to tell you. I don't think I'll come to work today."

"Why, honey," he said. He gave a start of interest. "Why —what's the matter?"

"It isn't anything," Mona said. She raised a reassuring smile. "I'm all right. I just don't feel very good."

"Oh," he said, and blushed. He thought he understood. "Well, that's a shame."

"I'm all right," she said. She tried to feel a sense of guilt, and couldn't. She had no real role in his life. The moment had come and gone in the undertaker's limousine. He had chosen *Foley's* instead. She was free to give her loyalty where it was needed. "I'll be fine," she said. "I just don't feel like working."

"Well," he said. He gave her an uncertain look. But he had nothing to add but his smile. He smiled.

"I know," she said. "So run along. You'll be late."

He patted her arm.

"I guess I'd better," he said, and brushed a kiss on her forehead.

"It's almost noon," she said.

He let her propel him gently toward the door. But he wasn't ready yet. A magazine cover caught his eye. He stopped and stared, and wandered on to the desk. He opened and closed a drawer. She prayed for time and patience. He loosened his belt a notch. It was as though he still had something more to say. But she knew he hadn't. It was just his way. He began to whistle again, and stuck his head into the closet. But habit made waiting no easier. He could hardly have lingered longer had she chosen to tell him the truth. She watched him rummaging among the hooks and hangers, and wondered what it really was that had made her hold it back. It wasn't only to avoid the certain flood of questions. It wasn't even because Leland had made her promise. It was something else. He emerged from the closet with his hat in his hand. Every distraction had been explored and exhausted. He was finally on his way. He fixed her with his broadest smile, and it gave her the answer she wanted. She couldn't tell him the truth. This wasn't the time for that. He would be too interested. He would smile and talk and want to know everything, but he wouldn't really care. It would only be a larger distraction.

"Papa," she said.

He nodded, and unchained and opened the door.

"Well," he said. "Now take good care of yourself."

"Yes," she said. "All right, Papa. Good-by."

She closed the door with the last of her patience. He had said thirty minutes. There could hardly be fifteen left. She ran wildly down the passage with her robe trailing wildly behind.

It was impossible to decide what dress to wear. She gazed into the closet and put out a hand at random. It came away with three. One was the dress she had worn the night they had found the secluded lane on the road to Shawnee Mission. The memory made her tremble. It was like an omen. She slipped it quickly over her head, and tumbled the others into her overnight bag. But she would need something more than dresses. She raked a comb through her hair, and emptied out her dressing-table drawers. The room already had a vacant look. When she came out of the closet with a hat on her head and a pair of shoes in her hand, it was stripped of everything that mattered. There was nothing left but the waste and the want and the waiting.

She gave the room a frantic final glance, and picked up the case. The feel of it was astonishing. It seemed to have no weight at all. She carried it along to the living-room as easily as her pocketbook, and wondered if there could be something that she had forgotten to pack. But everything she needed lay ahead, and nothing could make her return to the bedroom. The decision was as certain and as final as her love. She sat down at the desk and got out a sheet of paper and a pencil. She stared out the window, and tried to think. The woman in the apartment below was stretching clothes on a line. Three sparrows dodged among the leaves in the persimmon tree next door. Above the yard and above the tree, the sky was a blinding blue. She touched the pencil to her tongue, and shivered. *Dear Papa,* she wrote. *I'm afraid this is going to be quite a surprise . . .*

There was a sudden knock on the door. She almost jumped. She had been listening for the bell. She folded the paper and thrust it into an envelope and propped it against the lamp. There was another, harder, knock. She walked slowly across the room and slowly released the lock. He ducked into the room like a fugitive. She sank silently into his arms.

For a moment they stood silently together. Then he lifted her gently away.

"Look," he said. "Maybe we'd better—" He glanced quickly around the room. "Is everything all right? Has he gone?"

She tried to speak, and couldn't. It was incredible, but she was going to cry. She said, "There isn't anybody—" She gave a despairing whimper. The tears welled helplessly up. "Except you."

"I know," he said. "But that isn't any reason to cry." He gave a kind of laugh. "I mean, we aren't even married yet."

"Oh, damn," she said. "Damn. Damn."

"Don't," he said, and took her in his arms again. "Please don't."

"No," she said. "I won't any more. I'm all right." She turned her face away. "But don't kiss me. Not now. I'm too wet and awful."

"All right," he said. "But look—are you all ready? We've got to get going."

"Yes," she said. "I'm ready." She felt for a handkerchief and dabbed her eyes. "I guess that's why I was crying. I'm so damned ready."

"Well," he said, and hesitated. "No." He shook himself. "Tell me where your bag is and I'll get it."

"I don't know," she said. "It's somewhere. Over by the desk, I think."

She watched him bound across the room.

"I look awful, don't I?" she said. "I know I do. I must."

"Don't be silly," he said. He picked up the case and came bounding back. "You look wonderful. Like a bride."

"I wish I did," she said. "But I don't. I've got such a silly face. Even Papa—"

He said sharply, "You didn't tell him?"

"No," she said. "I was only talking about my face. He used to joke about— No, I didn't tell him. I wouldn't even if you hadn't made me promise. It was hard enough to write him a note."

"I know," he said. "I wrote one, too. But a note is enough. It's all that's necessary."

"It's funny," she said. "I mean, it's odd. I don't think I'd want to tell anybody. At least, until—"

"Of course not," he said. "It's nobody's damn business."

"It's just ours," she said. "It's just ours together. Isn't it?"

"That's right," he said.

It wasn't enough.

"Lee," she said. She put out her arms and drew him close against her. "I don't care if I do look awful. Lee— Oh, darling."

"Yes," he said. "But—" It was as formal as a handshake. He hardly touched her lips. "We've got to get moving," he said. "There's no use taking any chances."

"No," she said. She supposed he was right. She let him go.

"Have you got everything?" he said. "Hadn't you better take a coat or something? You can't be sure this time of year."

"It's on the sofa," she said.

"Good," he said. He caught it up and flung it over his arm. "Is that everything? Okay. You go ahead. I'll close the door."

He caught up with her in the hall, and clutched her arm. She turned quickly to him. But that wasn't what he meant. He only wanted her to hurry. He rushed her down the stairs. At the bottom, he abruptly halted.

"Wait," he said.

He hoisted the case into the hollow of his arm and covered it with her coat. Then he cautiously drew back the door. He looked carefully up and down the street.

"What's the matter?" she said.

"All right," he said. "Let's go."

"But what's the matter?" she said.

"Nothing," he said. "It's okay." He waved her through the door. "But just walk casually—the way you always do. As if we were just going for a ride or something."

"But why?" she said. It was bewildering. "I don't understand."

"Try to smile," he said. "Everybody's watching. We don't want them to— I mean, there's no point in advertising."

"Oh," she said. She had forgotten. Secrecy was the essence of any elopement. It could only be accomplished by stealth. She felt a kind of relief. "I didn't think," she said. "No—of course not."

"That's the ticket," he said.

They reached the car. He opened the door and heaved her bag onto the shelf beside his own. He backed awkwardly out and threw a quick glance over his shoulder.

"Okay," he said.

He left her standing on the curb. She watched him dart around the front of the car. He slid through the door and under the wheel. The engine started with a roar. He hardly waited until she was down in her seat. They spurted away from the curb in a splatter of dust and gravel. She looked involuntarily back. They had already turned the corner. A postman came out of the drugstore with an ice-cream cone in his hand.

She said, "Lee."

He gave her a short, abstracted glance.

"I just happened to think," she said. "I don't even know where we're going."

"Where?" he said.

"Yes," she said. "You didn't tell me on the phone. All you said was—"

"New Barton," he said.

"Oh," she said. "Where is that?"

He didn't answer. His eyes were fixed on the rear-vision mirror. He might not even have heard.

FIVE

A HEAVY TRUCK AND TRAILER burst over the rise ahead and stamped like thunder across the bridge. It charged whining down upon them with a glitter of sun on the windshield, and was past in a wild whip of wind. Then they were on the bridge and over it and dropping violently down the hill. The highway leveled out again on an endless plain of meadow and pasture and field. In the distance a ribbon of green marked the wandering course of a creek.

Leland took his foot off the accelerator. Speed died slowly away in a startling surge of silence. An encampment of corn swung sluggishly back toward the bridge. The car lurched off the slab. They crawled along the shoulder in a slap and snap of weeds. Beyond a limp wire fence a grizzled mule stood like a monument in the shade of a drooping elm.

"Ah," Leland said, and cut the engine. "Now then."

"What?" Mona said. She sat up in the seat and blinked. The feel of speed and motion dissolved in a blast of heat. It was like coming awake. "What are we stopping for? There isn't anything the matter?"

He plucked a cigarette from his pocket. He struck a match and grinned. "Not any more," he said. He flung the match away. "Didn't you see that sign a minute ago?"

"What sign?" she said.

"That boundary sign," he said. "You are now entering

Johnson County. We're across the line." He twisted around to the shelf behind the seat. "Which calls for a drink."

"I must have been asleep," she said. "But I still don't— Oh. You mean—"

"I mean, it's time to celebrate," he said. He sat back with a pint of whisky in his hand. "This is a big moment in my life."

"Your life?" she said. "What about me?" She looked at him with love and wonder. "Oh, Lee—I've been so afraid. Ever since we left home, I've had such an awful feeling. But you're glad, aren't you? You're really glad?"

"Glad?" he said. "Glad?" He gave a whoop of laughter. "I hope to God I'm—" He held the bottle up to the light and shook it, and laughed again. "Here. Have a cigarette. Have a drink. Mona, when I think of how long—"

His cigarette fell from his hand. He tumbled her hilariously to him. He mussed her hair and bit her ear and started to unbutton her dress. She had never, even on the road to Shawnee Mission, seen him like this before. But nothing was surprising any more. She went limp with happiness in his arms.

He sat suddenly up. He reached across her sprawling legs and snapped a switch. The radio in the dashboard leaped alive. A military band erupted into the car.

"How's that?" he said, and pounded out the beat on her thigh.

A station wagon shot past on the highway, as soundless as a shadow in the thundering, screaming, drumming bedlam of the music. He reached under her hip and brought out the bottle again and began to unscrew the cap. She pulled down her skirt and pulled up her brassière. He held the bottle invitingly out.

"Lee," she said. She raised her voice. "I can't—" But there was no use trying to talk against the *Stars and Stripes Forever.*

She squirmed away and felt for the dial and tuned the radio down. "You know I can't drink out of a bottle."

"Sure you can," he said. "I showed you that time."

"That was a Coke," she said.

"All right," he said. "I'll show you again. All you have to do is—"

He swallowed and choked and blinked, and thrust the bottle into her hand. A smell of whisky filled the car. It was as hot as the sun and as loud as the music. She had a wild and wonderful sense of debauchery.

He said, faintly, "I thought I had a cigarette."

"You did," she said, and giggled. "That's it on the floor by your foot."

"Good," he said. He picked it up and removed a hair and stuck it in his mouth. "Go on. Drink up."

"I don't think I can," she said. The mule regarded her from across the fence. "Not with that mule staring at me."

"Don't mind him," he said. "Just hold it with both hands and tip it up."

"I know," she said. "But—"

"You're not going to make me celebrate alone?" he said. "Go on now."

"Are we going to get drunk?" she said. "People do get drunk at weddings, don't they?"

"Always," he said. "Here— I'll even light a cigarette for you. So you won't strangle."

"I don't mind if we get tight," she said. "I mean, a little bit. We've never been married before, have we?"

"Drink up," he said. "Before you get too drunk."

"All right," she said. She laughed at his laughing face. "You think you're smart, don't you? Well—"

She raised the bottle, took a deep breath, and closed her eyes. The whisky blazed down her throat, and opened like a fan in her stomach. She clapped the cigarette to her mouth and shuddered and pushed the bottle away.

"Ugh," she said, and writhed against his chest.

He thumped her cheerfully on the back, and howled.

She leaned back and looked at him. He tilted up the bottle.

"Well?" she said.

He swallowed and shook his head and reached blindly for her cigarette.

"You do think you're smart," she said. "Don't you?"

He grinned. "Don't you?" he said.

She smiled at his happy face, at the shrilling music, at the staring mule in the field. A car with a Utah license and a flapping rear fender went plodding by. She included it in her smile.

"I love you," she said, and took the cigarette from his hand. "So I suppose I do."

SIX

N<small>EW</small> B<small>ARTON</small> <small>STRAGGLED OUT TO MEET THE HIGHWAY</small>: three billboards and a filling station, a store-front tabernacle and a junk yard, the gaping basement of a gutted house, a grocery store, and a row of clapboard bungalows. The concrete slab gave way to a lumpy, tree-lined street. Through the trees the late-afternoon sky shimmered like hammered brass. A man in an undershirt sat on the door-step of one of the houses with his head in his hands and a dog asleep at his feet.

"Well." Leland sat, and waved a hand. "Here we are. This is it."

"It's nice," Mona said. "I never saw such a nice town."

She peered unsteadily at the battered houses and the slumping trees. Her face felt as stiff as wax. She smiled and it seemed to crack.

"I guess I'd better turn off the radio," he said. "We don't want to sound like a parade."

"You know something?" she said. "I think I'm tight. Will the preacher like it if I'm tight?"

"He isn't a preacher," he said. "He's—" The car bumped over a traffic button. "He's a judge. I mean, a justice of the peace."

"Is that better?" she said. The image of the car and her staring face glided across the windows of a J. C. Penney store. "Don't judges mind? I didn't really mean to get tight. But we drank almost half the bottle."

"So what?" he said. "I've got another bottle. Besides, you aren't tight. You're all right. We're both all right."

"Umm," she said, and tucked her arm in his. "We are, aren't we?" It was as though he had finally declared his love. "We're both wonderful. Even if we are a little bit tight. But that's only because we're celebrating. So it's perfectly all right. Just so he isn't a preacher. I don't care about a judge or whatever he is."

"Justice of the peace," he said.

The street ran into a somnolent square. In the center of the square, in a grove of cottonwood trees, stood a Civil War cannon and a pyramid of black iron balls. Around the square, facing the Rexall Drug Store and the A. & P. and Rudy's Recreation Parlor and the Peabody Furniture Mart and the ten-cent store and the First National Bank and the Mikado Theater, was a ragged rank of parked cars. Leland nosed into the curb in front of the A. & P.

"You wait here," he said. "I'll be back in a minute."

"What for?" she said. "Where are you going? This isn't where we—?"

"I'll be right back," he said, and slammed the door.

She watched his dark head and his tan gabardine back dodging through the shirt sleeves and overalls and house dresses. Something distracted her, and when she looked again, he was gone. The shirt sleeves and overalls and house dresses streamed back and forth. In front of Rudy's a knot of leaning men guffawed. She wondered if she were the reason, and gazed contentedly back. That didn't matter any more. She was out of their reach forever.

Leland's voice said, "Hey. Open up."

He stood at the door, hugging an enormous sack. He grinned at her over a parapet of bags and parcels and boxes, and winked.

"Good heavens," she said. "What's that?"

"Food," he said, and shoved the sack back against the luggage on the shelf. Two oranges and a can of something rolled out. He let himself down on the seat and wiped his face with a folded handkerchief.

"So I see," she said. Another orange rolled out and across the shelf. "But what for?"

He started the car.

"We've got to eat," he said. "I was afraid the stores might be closed later on. It's past five now."

"I know," she said. "But—"

"I guess I forgot to tell you," he said. He stuck the handkerchief back in his pocket and gave her an anxious glance. "Here's the thing. We've got a hunting shack over in Cass County. I thought we might stay there tonight. It's only about fifteen miles from here. Nobody's used it since my father died and it isn't much of a place, but I thought it might be better than—"

"Lee." She stopped him with a whisper of surprise and delight. "Why didn't you tell me?" A memory of tourist camps and highway hotels fled drearily across her mind. She had a sense of relief so sharp that it could have been joy. "A place of our own," she said.

"Well," he said. "At least, there won't be anybody snooping around."

"No," she said. "Oh—it sounds wonderful. It's the most wonderful thing I ever heard of. And I'm glad you didn't tell me. I'm glad it was a surprise."

"To tell the truth," he said, "I just forgot. But I have got a surprise for you." He felt in his pocket. "It's what they call a wedding ring."

"Don't," Mona said. "Not yet." She closed her eyes and shook her head. "I don't want to see it now. It's bad luck."

"It's only from Kresge's," he said.

"That's my favorite store," she said. "But do as I say. Put it back in your pocket. I want to look at you."

"This is only for now," he said. "I'll get you a real one—well, the first chance I get."

"I don't want a real one," she said. "I mean, I don't want any other. That's the only one I want."

He laughed, and the car gave a lurch. She felt it swing

away from the curb and around.

"You'd better open your eyes," he said. "You'll get dizzy."

"I am dizzy," she said.

"I know you are," he said. "Or you wouldn't be here. But since you are, how about lighting me a cigarette?"

"You smoke too much," she said, and felt in his pocket for the package. "Now where are we going? Do you know where it is?"

"From now on," he said, "I'm going to have you light all my cigarettes. I like that raspberry lipstick flavor. I can't get enough of it."

"I hope not," she said. "But where are we going? Are we—?"

He nodded.

"It's just around the corner," he said. "I looked it up back there. He has his office in his house."

The house was in the middle of the first block off the square. It stood behind a picket fence in a sunken yard overgrown with tiger lilies, and was tall and turreted and painted a liverish brown. A red-white-and-blue sign was suspended from the porch railing. It read: *Fred B. Weaver, Justice of the Peace. Licenses Issued & Marriages Performed. Day & Night Service.* There was an empty beer can under a bush beside the gate.

"Well," Leland said, and turned off the engine.

"It looks haunted," she said.

"It does at that," he said. He gave an uneasy laugh, and opened the gate. "However . . ."

He took her arm as they went up the walk. She had a feeling someone was watching from behind a shade in an upper window. They climbed the steps and halted at a baggy screen door. There was a smell of something cooking. In the half-dark inside the door, a straw hat hung like a face on the back of a ponderous wardrobe.

"Are you scared?" Mona said. "I am."

"There's nothing to be scared about," he said. He cleared his throat and pressed the bell. "Don't be silly."

"All right," she said. She caught his eye and nodded toward the cigarette in his hand. "Don't you think you ought to—?"

"Oh," he said. "Sure."

He turned and threw it away.

Somewhere a door closed softly.

A throaty voice said, "Good evening, young people."

A long dim face floated past the straw hat.

"Don't be shy," the voice said. "Step right in."

Leland said, "We're—"

"I think I can guess your little secret," the voice said, and chuckled. "So come right in."

A light went on, and a tall gray man with a sagging face and a dozen chins backed smiling away from the door. His hair was thin and the color of skin and it hung halfway down his neck. He had on a dark jacket and gray trousers and a blue work shirt and a flowing Windsor tie. Arranged in his breast pocket was a row of yellow pencils.

"Permit me to introduce myself," he said. "I'm Judge Weaver."

"How do you do," Leland said. "I— My name is—"

"Of course," Judge Weaver said. "But first." He waved a long gray hand. "May I suggest we—"

They followed him past the wardrobe and into a small white room. There was a table in the middle of the room and around the walls were chairs and two leather couches. It might have been a dentist's outer office. A caramel was melting beside a cigar butt in an ash tray on a wrought-iron stand. There was a photograph of three bearded men in a rowboat on one wall. On another was a framed illustrated poem.

"Now, little lady," Judge Weaver said. "If you will just—"

He hovered over her, smiling and frowning and panting, like a photographer. She found herself sitting on the edge of a creaking chair. He spun nimbly around and clapped Leland on the shoulder. She watched them cross the room and bend solemnly over the table. The framed poem was just above her head. She turned and looked at it. It read:

No one knows but Mother and Dad,
About the smiles and tears we've had.
No other is willing and glad to share,
Whatever we have of joy . . .

Judge Weaver recalled her with a murmur.

"Allow me," he said.

She let herself be led down the room. A door opened and a swarthy woman in a red dress and gold earrings came in. She posted herself against the wall like a sentry. Mona glanced at Leland. He was staring carefully at nothing. Judge Weaver cleared his throat. He began to speak in a rapid, rambling mumble. His long face swung this way and that. The chins bounced up and down before her eyes.

"Say 'I will,' " Judge Weaver said.

She heard herself say, "I will."

The woman at the door blew her nose.

"I now pronounce you husband and—"

Silence filled the room. Judge Weaver breathed, and waited. Leland stirred and swallowed.

"Wife," Judge Weaver said.

He lowered his head. Silence returned again. Then the woman coughed and vanished through the door.

"I wish you every happiness," Judge Weaver said.

Mona stared at the cold silver ring on her finger.

"Thank you," Leland said. He hesitated, and brought out his billfold. "I—"

"Anything you wish to give," Judge Weaver said. He smiled. "I could ask you for what the little lady is worth." He chuckled. "But I'm afraid you couldn't afford that much."

"No," Leland said, and seemed to be trying to smile. He opened his billfold. "But—"

Judge Weaver glanced at the ten-dollar bill and thrust it into his pocket. With another smile he swept them adroitly to the door.

"I wish you every happiness," he said.

"Yes," Leland said. "Thanks. Thank you very much."

"Thank you," Mona said, and hardly knew her voice.

The screen door closed behind them. Nothing moved on the street. The sun was almost down, and on either side of the walk the tiger lilies flared in the dusk.

Leland started to speak, and didn't. She silently took his hand. Marriage had left them with nothing to say to each other.

SEVEN

Leland TILTED THE LAST DRIBBLE OF WHISKY into his coffee. He shook his head and laughed.

"Well, young people," he said.

He had forgotten to buy kerosene for the lamps, and the candle flames reached like fingers up the walls and among the cobwebs on the ceiling. Through the windows they could hear the river sighing past the willows at the foot of the bluff. There was a smell of damp from the water and the night and the years the shack had stood empty.

"But he did marry us," Mona said.

"Anything you wish to give," he said. "You saw him grab that money." He said with tolerant contempt, "He's like all the rest of them."

The long room that they had swept to bareness flickered in the wavering light: the dying fire in the big stone fireplace, the cans and packages of food on the shelves between the windows, the two iron cots in the far corner, the Navajo rug on the floor, the pouting blonde on the 1932 calendar. It was like another world.

"There aren't any of the rest of them now," Mona said. She pushed her plate away. "I don't believe there is anybody but us."

"No," he said, and took a gulp of coffee. "And that's the way it's going to stay."

"You mean, here?" she said. "Oh, Lee—let's. Let's do.

Let's don't go back for a long time." Her father fell out of her mind like the past. He was as far away as Ritchie. "We'll just live here. Could we, Lee?"

"Sure," he said. "Of course we can. We'll stay here as long as we please." He lighted a cigarette. "Then we'll go somewhere else. Mexico, maybe."

"I don't want to go any place else," she said. No other place could ever be so completely their own. "Not for a long time, anyway. Not for weeks."

He waved solemnity away and leaned across the table and cupped her chin in his hand.

"I always kiss my little brides," he said. "If they're pretty."

"I'll say you do," she said. "But he didn't say that."

"Yes, he did," he said.

"I was his little bride," she said. "But he didn't say it."

"All right," he said. "He didn't. I thought he would, though. I was sure he would. I can't imagine why he didn't. Unless it was because of that woman."

Mona giggled.

"I thought he was going to, too," she said.

"The old bastard," he said.

"Lee," she said.

"All right," he said. "I take it back. He wasn't so old at that."

"He was too old for me," she said.

"He was too everything for you," he said.

"Everybody is," she said. "Everybody but you."

"Fine," he said. "Then allow me—"

He bounded around the table. A spoon clattered to the floor. She kicked it away with her foot, and raised her face to his.

"Delicious," he said, and bounded away.

"I wish you could see your face," she said. "I'm going to have to stop wearing lipstick." She straightened her dress, and a button came away in her hand. "And clothes," she said.

"I like you in lipstick," he said. "You know, I wish we

had some music. I feel like dancing."

"Dancing?" she said. "I thought you— Marriage has certainly changed you."

"I'm a wonderful dancer," he said. "Just watch me."

"You're a wonderful everything," she said.

"I know," he said. "But I do better with a partner. Be my partner, little lady."

He had never been so silly. She had never loved him more. He came waltzing back to the table.

"Lee," she said. "You nut."

"Allow me," he said, and pulled back her chair.

She stood weakly up. The room was suddenly stifling. She let him dance her down the room. The candles shook like her heart. He nuzzled his face in her hair and bit her ear, and whispered.

"Yes," she said. "But—"

They stumbled against a cot.

"Aha," he said. "Just what—"

The bed bumped against the wall. He pulled her toward it. They fell sprawling across the mattress.

"Mona—"

"Yes," she said. "Oh, Lee. Oh, my darling . . ."

She threw herself against him. A piece of his shirt ripped loose in her hand. She cried out again in a kind of agony, and tried to find his mouth.

EIGHT

Leland lifted himself exhausted from the pillow. It was as though he hadn't slept at all. A gray, watery light dripped like rain through the windows. And it was raining —a thin, lifeless, enervating rain that floated down as fine as fog. He could hear it dripping on the roof and seeping through the trees. In the distance, at the foot of the bluff, the river murmured and sighed. He supposed it was morning.

His strength gave out. He lay heavily back, hugging the blanket to his chin. It was almost cold. Beside him in the narrow cot, Mona stirred and whimpered, and sank deeper into sleep. He moved a hand and felt for her breast. But the impulse dribbled away. That wasn't what he wanted. He was too tired and tense and dispirited for that. He wanted— He didn't know what he wanted. A ripple of pain rolled up from the back of his head and settled behind his eyes. There was no more hope of sleep. He might as well get up.

He crawled drearily out of bed and stood shivering on the cold, bare floor. A mounted trout stared coldly down from the mantel. Their clothes were tangled together in and around a chair. He probed through the evidence of happiness with a kind of amazement. It was hard to believe that only last night he had actually felt like that. It might have been a lifetime ago. He found his underwear under her slip and his trousers in a heap on the floor. His shirt was torn from cuff to elbow, and the collar was smeared with what he supposed was lipstick. But it was too much trouble to try to find his suitcase and a clean one. He put it on and buttoned it up, and looked glumly around for his shoes. His mind hung as limp as the ripped and dangling sleeve.

He clumped across the room with his shoelaces trailing. Everything was damp. It was like moving under water. The fish swam past him on its mounting. A bottle slithered away from his foot like something half alive. The remains of last night's supper lay scattered on the table like something thrown up by a tide. They hadn't remembered to close the door. He stepped over a puddle and onto the stoop. The flags of the walk sat islanded in muddy water. His car stood in a marsh of weeds in the lee of a roofless shed. It wasn't as early as he had thought. Something that could have been the sun glowed now and then through a tear in the woolen sky. The rain dripped coldly down his face. He turned listlessly back into the house.

He couldn't understand what had happened. He dropped down in a damp chair and lighted a damp cigarette. The smoke hung like an expiring balloon in the air. He felt aged and altered overnight. Nothing was the same. Nothing was right. He threw the cigarette into the fireplace. It was as though it were somehow to blame. There was nothing and nobody else. He had rid himself of everyone but the only one that mattered. They had all been left behind. He was in Cass County, out of their sight and reach. He shook himself and stood aimlessly up. It was possible that some coffee would help. Or a drink. Indecision trapped him between the table and the shelf. He didn't really want either. They weren't enough to dislodge the lump of depression. Mona sighed and turned over in the bed. A bare arm crept slowly across the blanket. The ring on her finger caught a spark of light. He looked doubtfully down at his wife. But he had no regrets about that. He told himself uneasily that he had no regrets about anything. He had left nothing behind that mattered, and he was surrounded by love and safety. No one in the world knew where he was. They hadn't seen him come here, and they wouldn't see him leave. He might, for all they knew, be still in— His name darted at him, scribbled on the official paper. Marriage had charted the direction of his escape. The trail was blazed to New Barton. He was known to a justice of the peace.

He walked quickly to the door, and slowly back again. But there was no reason to worry about New Barton. The justice of the peace had hardly glanced at either his name or his face. He had been interested only in his fee. But doubt still sat in a corner of his mind. He felt it there like the watching face of the detective. The pain behind his eyes rose and fell, like a pulse. He told himself that he had done the only thing he could. He had got away before they had what they needed. It was unlikely that even his mother would imagine that this was where he had come. But even if she did— He turned for distraction to the window. From the rear of the house the woods fell steeply away to the river. He watched the swollen water running brown and heavy through a filigree of willows. On the far shore the blacktop road to the highway wound like patent leather through brushy fields toward the bridge.

He began to whistle confidence back. His uneasiness was only the weather. It was a reaction from yesterday's excitement. It was the unfamiliar feel of freedom. Everything had been settled yesterday morning. All of the alternatives had been explored and defined and discarded in that hour of cold reflection on the park bench. He had seen their trap in time, and reason had shown him the only road to safety. He had broken out beyond their reach. They had nothing left but their empty guilty hands. The thought was encouraging. He tried to imagine what they would think or do. Hope tempted him on. What could they do? He was their essential witness. They had gambled everything on his testimony. But he had refused to testify against himself. He had refused to convict . . .

Doubt suddenly stirred in its corner. It moved and gathered strength, burst ablaze into panic. He stumbled out of the chair as if they were already at the door. But it was inconceivable. This was a honeymoon. He thanked God hopelessly that he had used his right name. The justice of the peace at New Barton could give the proof. They couldn't make anyone believe that he had run away in guilt. This couldn't be the last false link of evidence. This couldn't be what they had watched and waited and hounded him for. This couldn't be the hidden design in their strategy. He couldn't have made the final fatal mistake. But he had. He had. He knew beyond question that he had.

The Navajo rug caught at his feet.

"Mona—"

He wrenched the blankets to the floor.

"*Mona*—wake up!"

Mona plunged up to horror, fighting instinctively back. Something dragged her into space. She fell to her knees beside the bed.

"What is it?" She began to scream. "Papa—"

A wild face hung over her. A wild voice babbled. She crouched frozen on the floor, and stared at the shape of consciousness.

It wasn't a dream. She was awake. The knowledge doubled her terror. She tried to crawl away.

Somebody pulled her up. It was Lee. She tottered against the bed and sat down. This was the hunting shack. It was morning. But what had happened?

Leland gave a groan and shook her shoulders. Panic blazed in his eyes. His hand on her flesh was ice.

". . . the police."

It was the first of his words she could understand.

"But there's still time," he said. "Only we've got to hurry."

He leaped frantically across the room.

Fright fell slowly away to bewilderment. She became

aware of the drip of rain, and suddenly of cold. Her feet touched the tumbled blanket.

"Here—"

An armful of clothes fell into her lap: a stocking, a dress, a brassiere, a gabardine jacket. She pushed them aside and drew the blanket up around her.

He was down on his knees, tying his shoes.

"Lee," she said. "What is it? What's happened? I—"

"I told you," he said. "I just got through telling you. It'll take them time to find this place, but they've had all night. They've had more than twelve hours. And the way they work—"

"Who?" she said. She tried to calm herself. It wasn't as though he had never acted strangely before. "Who's trying to find us? You don't think Papa—"

"All of them," he said. He rose up and took a tottering step. "The police, and all the rest of them."

He sank down on the cot as if the words had emptied him.

He said heavily, "Oh, God. You don't know. I forgot you didn't know. I didn't think there was any need. I thought everything would be—all right."

She sat as cold as the rain at the window, with a clammy blanket around her and a clammy stocking in her hand.

"But Lee—"

He swept her voice aside.

"Listen," he said. "Listen and I'll try to . . ."

The words spewed out in an appalling flood. She clutched the stocking as though it stood for reason and reality. His whole deluded world was revealed like a sudden malignancy. She sat surrounded by suspicion and hate and brutality.

"But Lee," she said. "That's Ritchie's station. He—"

"Ritchie?" he said. "Okay. But what difference does his name make? He was only one of them."

There was no way to stop the awful, tormented flow. His voice roved back and forth through the months. His mind held the memory of everything. She wanted to turn away and stop her ears, but the hot, sick eyes held her through all the intricate and elaborate fabrications.

He said, "You were the only one. People I've known all my life. My friends. And at the bank. My father's best friend. Even my mother, I think. All except you, Mona. You were the only one."

"Yes," she said. She wondered why she wasn't frightened. But she felt only sad and weak with pity. She moved across the bed to be close to him. He pushed away.

"You do know?" he said. "You do understand? But there's nothing for you to be frightened about. They're not interested in you. I'm the only one. But that's all right. Because we've still got time. We'll get away. We'll find a place. Don't worry about that. And also—I promise you they'll never get me. Never."

"No," she said.

"Maybe they'll even find out who really did it," he said. "They might. I mean, in spite of themselves."

"Yes," she said.

It wasn't really a surprise. She had a sense that something like this had lain hidden in her mind from the first. All that he had really told her now was the cause of all his strangeness. She thought with a kind of awe: *I'm the only one that knows. I'm the only one he would ever trust.* She looked at him with the beginning of understanding. Madness wasn't screaming and fighting and wild grimaces. It was only an enormous seriousness. It was sitting on the edge of a cot and believing something that wasn't true.

"I am the only one," she said. She was the only hope he had. This was the real test of her vocation. She alone knew the way to reality. "I am the only one. Aren't I?"

Leland felt a vast relief in having told her everything. She now knew all that he had struggled against alone. She now knew his singlehanded strength. The dead weight of exhaustion had gone. His head was clear. He felt equal to any of them now.

He gazed for a moment through the window at the

river and the road and the fields beyond. In the distance
the surging water muttered at the pilings of the bridge.
It might have been the sound of an approaching car. The
sound recalled him to danger.

He scrambled off the bed.

"Ready?" he said.

"Practically," Mona said. She stood up, smoothing the
dress over her hips, and fastened her belt. "Why don't you
light the fire so I can get the coffee started."

"Coffee?" he said. He stiffened. "Are you crazy? We
haven't got time for coffee. We haven't got time for anything. We've got to get going."

"We can't leave without breakfast," she said. "Besides,
you said we could stay here. You said we didn't have to
leave for a long—"

"That was yesterday," he said. He almost gagged on impatience. "That was before I realized. Mona—for God's
sake! They could be here any minute."

"I know," she said. "But they won't. They won't find us
here. If we just stay here, I know—"

"Mona," he said. "Listen to me. You don't know them.
You don't know how they work."

"No," she said. "But—"

He hadn't the strength to go through it all again, and
there wasn't time. It was like talking to someone who
didn't know the language.

He said, "Don't you think I know what I'm talking
about? Don't you think I know them? Good God, I've
been—" The warning murmur rose again from the river.
"We've got to get out of here."

"Lee," she said, and reached for his hand. "We can't. We
mustn't. Darling—we are safe here. This is the safest place
in the world."

He pushed her hand aside. Exasperation blinded him.
He jerked her away from the bed and sent her stumbling
toward the table.

"I'm not going to argue with you," he said. "If you
haven't got sense enough to—"

She gave a wail of fright and caught the edge of the table. "Lee—"

"Come on," he said. "I said we were going and I mean it." He raised a threatening hand. "If you think I'm going to wait here like a mouse—" He gave her a shove. "Get going."

She broke away. Her heel caught in the rug and a shoe fell off. She backed against the fireplace.

"Wait," she said. "Listen. Darling—listen to me, please. There isn't anybody coming. There isn't anybody ever coming. There isn't anything to be afraid of."

He halted, cold and dead and staring. She didn't understand. The thought sank numbly through him. She didn't understand a thing. And there was no more time. He had wasted all he had. He stood helpless with dismay. Even she had failed him.

"No," he said.

"Lee," she said. "I love you. I—"

Dismay erupted into rage.

"Shut up!"

"I won't," she said. "I can't. You've got to—"

"Shut up!"

"Lee—"

"Okay," he said. His car was waiting in the yard. He wouldn't be trapped by someone else's stupidity. "Stay here, then."

He started for the door.

But she was there ahead of him, standing crookedly in one shoe, blocking the way. Her face collapsed in tears. She caught at his coat.

"No." She choked. "Lee, darling. No. No—"

He butted her through the doorway. She clung to his coat.

"Get out of my way."

She cried, "No. I won't. You *can't!*"

"*No?*"

Panic threw his fist. The wet wood slipped under her feet like ice. She went backward down the steps. He caught his balance against the side of the doorway, and heard the thud of her head on stone.

Nothing moved but his heart.

He looked at her staring rigidly up at the rain. But it wasn't the end. It was only the beginning. He had never known until now the full hurricane force of terror. They had stripped him of his strength and his friend—and his innocence. He had nothing left but his cunning.

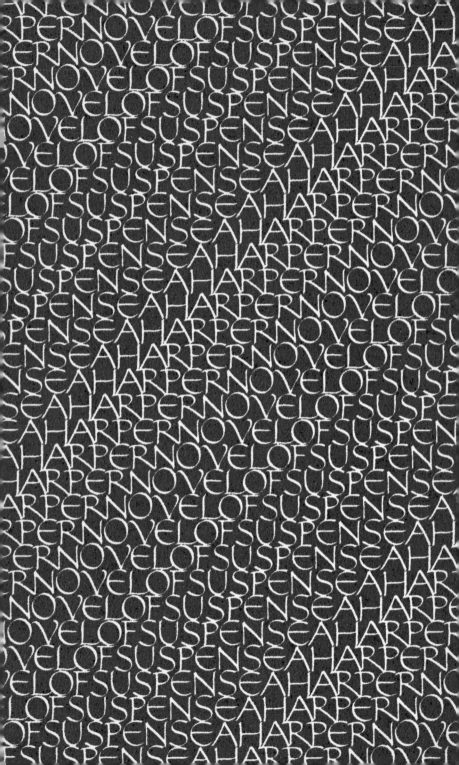